LOOKING FOR LAURIE

On finding a dead body in her flat, Laurie Kendal fights her instinct to scream, and instead races to the nearest police station. About to embark upon a cycling holiday, DI Tom Jessop attends the scene, only to find . . . nothing! The body has inexplicably disappeared, and so he dismisses Laurie's story as rubbish. But there is something intriguing about Laurie — she is beautifully eccentric, yet vulnerable too, and earnest in her insistence that her story is true. So before starting his holiday, Tom has one more check on her flat . . .

BETH JAMES

LOOKING FOR LAURIE

Complete and Unabridged

LINFORD
Leicester

First published in Great Britain in 2014

First Linford Edition
published 2015

*A catalogue record for this book is available
from the British Library.*

ISBN 978–1–4448–2659–3

Published by
F. A. Thorpe (Publishing)
Anstey, Leicestershire

Set by Words & Graphics Ltd.
Anstey, Leicestershire
Printed and bound in Great Britain by
T. J. International Ltd., Padstow, Cornwall

This book is printed on acid-free paper

1

Afterwards, Laurie wondered how she could possibly have felt so light-hearted as she'd made her way home from work at the unusually early hour of one o'clock. How, gazing at the Underground map on the opposite wall, she could ever have swayed to the train's movement in the heat-laden atmosphere, thinking only of the bottle of cool white wine sitting in her fridge just waiting to be opened. She remembered planning what she would wear that evening after they eventually stopped with the talking, the reminiscing and the catching up, and finally went out into the sultry evening air for something to eat.

London, once the commuters had gone, could be quite magical. Laurie had pictured the two of them, Gemma and herself, sauntering down the road in the semi-twilight to where, just a couple of blocks away, an area of eating places and late-night shops would be open well into the early hours. The place would be buzzing with all nationalities. There would be all styles of dress, many different accents, and everything would be just so cool. So London! Although Gemma had never been a close friend, Laurie still looked forward to the prospect of showing her around.

The train jerked to a halt. Laurie stepped onto the platform and walked with her fellow passengers towards the exit. The air outside was fractionally cooler. Gratefully, she took a couple of lungfuls and hummed a few bars of the song that had been going round in her head all day. It was a song that had been popular at the time when she had been bidding farewell to South Africa and Gemma, and contemplating real life again in London.

She felt herself smiling as she recalled her last night in Jo'berg. The goodbyes and the 'any time you're in London's that flowed so freely from her lips to all and sundry. OK, so it was rather sooner than she'd intended and a surprise, but surely a welcome surprise to hear from Gemma so quickly. And after all, Gemma had come to her rescue when she'd needed her, hadn't she? When Laurie had suddenly found herself homeless in Jo'berg she had opened the door to her small, two-roomed apartment with a smile and a 'sure you can stay — that's what mates are for.'

Yes, Gemma had been more than generous and Laurie had been humbled and grateful because deep inside she'd known that actually in the past, they'd never really warmed to each other. She didn't really know why it should be so, only that there was rather too much openness in Gemma's demeanour, her laughter a trifle forced and too hearty to be convincing. Then Laurie had told herself she was being too English; that Gemma's lack of reserve was the South African way.

And that had proved to be the case.

Because in the end Gemma had come up trumps, putting Laurie up at a nominal rent for a month while she found her feet again after her busted romance, busted career, and busted life really. Then when Laurie had got herself together again and saved enough for her return to London, going on to help with her travel arrangements, even offering to accompany her to the airport in a way Laurie found extraordinary, before saying a final goodbye.

Only it transpired that the goodbye was not final after all because, less than two months later, it seemed Gemma had arrived in the UK and was even now — having retrieved Laurie's spare key from under the mat as instructed — sitting in Laurie's flat ready for a grand reunion.

Laurie's step quickened as she came in sight of the block of purpose-built but shoebox-sized flats where she lived. It would be fun. She was sure it would be fun. Just so long as the visit remained as brief as Gemma had inferred on the phone. Despite feeling she owed her, too much Gemma was not an idea she relished.

'Only a flying visit,' she'd said on the phone yesterday. 'I've got to carry on up north — visit boring relations, you know the sort of thing.'

Laurie had said 'sure' with a laugh that belied the fact that actually she quite clearly remembered Gemma telling her that she had no relatives, let alone any in England. Usually when you were abroad and people realised where you were from, the first thing they did was tell you the exact whereabouts of their relations, even down to the pub they frequented, in the irrational belief that somehow, out of the sixty million plus inhabitants of Great Britain, you might have bumped into them. But Gemma had made no such hopeful query.

Laurie shrugged. Gemma had her strange ways, but for all that it would be good to see her again. Soon she would hear all about whatever had been happening in Jo'berg. About Red and Jody, Clare and Brad; all the old crowd.

At the swing doors of the building, that remained unlocked in the daytime at least, Laurie paused and fished around in her rucksack for her keys. She frowned; tonight it seemed they were being deliberately elusive. As she walked through the downstairs foyer and up the stairs to the first floor landing where her flat was, she was still rooting through the everyday debris that lined her rucksack. Just as she reached her front door her fingers closed over the metal of her keys, but her smile of triumph died on her lips when she realised the door was unlatched.

Strange.

Or, of course, not strange at all. Why should it be strange? She'd given Gemma instructions to let herself in and make herself at home. Maybe Gemma, hot and tired after her journey, had decided to take a shower and left the door unlatched for Laurie.

Perhaps she hadn't realised that in London you just didn't leave your door unlocked, *especially* if you were taking a shower. Goodness, hadn't Gemma ever seen *Psycho*?

But still, for some obscure reason, Laurie was reticent to call out the greeting that had been forming in her mind. Cautiously, she pushed the door wider and stepped into the small hallway.

'Hi.'

It was a man's voice. Laurie froze.

'No luck yet,' the voice continued. 'I've been disturbed.'

The owner of the voice was in the living room just out of Laurie's eyeshot. Aiming to keep it that way, she leaned back, desperately hoping he hadn't somehow spotted her.

'Unfortunate, really,' the mumble went on. 'I'll call in when I finish up.'

Careful to make no noise, Laurie backed out of the flat.

A series of conflicting emotions went through her. What on earth was going

7

on? What gave anyone the right to be in her flat? Why didn't she, coward that she was, just barge in there and ask what he was doing in her space?

For a long moment Laurie stood outside her front door contemplating doing just that. Righteously incensed, her stomach fluttered and her heart pounded with the beginnings of fury, but she couldn't ignore some sixth sense that was telling her very clearly to back off. Slowly she crept back down the stairs and into the foyer, where she loitered for a further moment wondering what to do.

Who was in her flat, and what was 'I've been disturbed' supposed to mean?

The obvious solution was that he'd heard her on the landing or coming up the stairs and because, owing to her search for her key, she hadn't immediately come into the flat, he'd thought she'd either gone on up the stairs to the next floor or into one of the other flats on her landing.

Laurie's heartbeat had nearly returned to normal. It was fairly evident now that she must have disturbed a burglar. Typical that a burglar would choose today to strike! She wondered how many other flats had been targeted. This was an old block dating back to the nineteen thirties; they really ought to get rid of the swing doors and install a proper locking device on a burglar-proof front door.

She gave herself a mental shake. It was probably only kids again. Then she frowned. The voice she'd heard certainly hadn't sounded like a kid's voice.

Well, a burglary, but by a professional, striking at mid-day when most people were out working. Maybe a gang? A dangerous gang. Thank goodness she'd made it home before Gemma arrived. Or maybe Gemma had arrived and gone out again to get some supplies in the form of wine and ciggies. Yes, that was probably it.

What was she doing? Why hadn't she phoned the police so they could catch the guy red-handed? Laurie shrugged her rucksack off her shoulder and reached into it for her phone. As she did so, she heard what sounded like her flat door closing, the noise of soft footsteps and the same man's voice as he spoke into his mobile.

Without thinking too much about it, she quickly and silently dived into the caretaker's cupboard and found herself squashed between a galvanised bucket containing a very smelly mop, and some form of unresisting cleaning equipment — probably the upright floor polisher the caretaker used. The door was cracked open enough to form a slim aperture through which she was able to see. The man's voice was easily audible as he approached down the stairs.

'Got it,' he said. 'The English girl — Laura was it? — disturbed me . . . Yep, damn nuisance . . . Don't worry, it's taken care of. Need a clean-up job though . . . '

In the cupboard Laurie bit her lip hard and concentrated on breathing quietly, or not breathing at all.

She was suddenly very afraid.

From her confined position all she could see was that he was large, with a shaved head and tattoos at the back of his neck: a snake, and what looked like a crocodile, fighting. Laurie's thoughts wavered towards the hysterical. Did snakes and crocodiles fight? What an absurd tattoo to have.

Just when he was level with the cupboard, he paused and the rucksack he had on his shoulder bumped against the cupboard door which shut with a definite and final-sounding click.

★   ★   ★

DI Thomas Jessop swung through the door to his work place. He'd just consumed a cheese and tomato sandwich — brown bread, not too much salt — followed by a mug of green tea. He usually had a bacon butty and strong breakfast tea with his colleagues but when, as today, he lunched alone, he

11

preferred to eat healthily. Tom predicted that this afternoon would be calm and peaceful, a time for sorting out paperwork and computer records, and checking that all relevant statements were signed correctly and filed accordingly, then making sure that things were running in an organised fashion before he took off tomorrow for his long-anticipated cycling trip.

His bike, his only friend on the trip, was in tip-top condition. Body oiled and polished, brakes adjusted perfectly, and tyres pumped to exactly the right pressure. For six wonderful days it would be just Tom, his machine and the open road before him. No hassle, no station squabbles, no cajoling sulky youths or calming hysterical parents, no tedious form-filling and, above all, an escape from the upper-management politics of policing.

If anyone had taken the trouble to ask him, DI Jessop would have said without hesitation that he loved his job. Serving the community was a people person's job and Tom, on the whole, was a people person. He liked to study the human species and figure out how they ticked, and over the years he thought he'd learned to judge a person's character pretty accurately; to know instinctively when a person was telling the truth and when they weren't. Of course there were all sorts of ways, textbook ways that he'd been taught at Hendon, which would point you in the right direction, but in reality it was just as portrayed on the television — gut instinct. Although by no means infallible, gut instinct was a thing that couldn't be learned. You either had it or you didn't. And Tom was pretty sure that most days he had it.

But right now all he hoped for was a hassle-free afternoon so that tomorrow he could head off, conscience clear, for the huge open skies of who knew where. Well, he did know where — roughly. Certainly north Essex, and then Suffolk — his conscience told him he owed a brief visit in that area — and maybe even on to Norfolk if time allowed. A smile pulled at the edge of his lips. Just him and his bike, a predominantly flat road for speed, with maybe the odd incline here and there, which would challenge him enough to make his muscles ache pleasantly at the end of the day.

Looking through the glass window of his office, he nodded at Detective Constable Judith Morgan who, looking neat and efficient in a trouser suit, was sitting at her desk. She gave him a cheery wave back before wrapping her hands round her coffee mug and turning her eyes back to her computer screen.

Tom pursed his lips. Yes, a bloke needed a bit of time on his own. A break away from work would be welcome. The only people he seemed to fraternise with lately were work mates and sometimes this could be danger- ous, especially when one of your work colleagues was as attractive as Judith Morgan. The last thing he wanted to do was hook up with someone just because of the proximity factor, and Tom was honest enough to admit that, although Judith was attractive and everyone in the station was laying bets that sooner or later the two of them would get together, for him, at least, there was something missing. What the something was, he had no idea, but until he did, he knew it wasn't fair to let the relationship develop — as it so easily could — into anything other than a 'good mates' friendship.

He wasn't looking for a relationship anyway. Not really. Only sometimes it would be nice to have somebody to talk to about something other than work; someone to share a joke with or, as a change from a pub, a meal in a good restaurant, or even a visit to the theatre.

A girlfriend in fact. A non-serious friendship with a girl. A girly girl who had nothing to do with policing, had never seen a dead body in her life, and still had an air of innocence about her. That quality of unworldliness Tom rarely recognised in any of the opposite sex whom he had dealings with these days.

But for now he was happy being single and therefore complication-free. Relationships were inevitably messy and Tom didn't like mess — he saw enough of it at work.

He switched on his computer and with a happy sigh clicked on the weather forecast for the east coast over the next few days.

* * *

Inside the cupboard everything was black. It was an all-enveloping blackness evoking the temptation to scream and shout and pound on the door.

Not the thing to do, Laurie. Keep calm. This too will pass.

With the utmost difficulty, because she really felt like yelling her head off, Laurie kept quiet and counted to twenty. By the time she reached fifteen, the guy outside the door had moved off again and she heard the street door open and close. Forcing herself to count slowly and calmly, Laurie started at one again. Two, three, four . . . She would not think about the fact that Snake-tattoo had mentioned her name — well Laura was too close to Laurie to be a coincidence; people had been calling her Laura by mistake for most of her life. She would not think, either, about him being in her flat and going through her things, as well as knowing her name. Right now she concentrated only on reaching twenty without dying of fright.

Twenty!

Laurie let go an expulsion of breath. He should be down the street by now and whatever it was he'd wanted, he'd said he'd got it. Hadn't he? He wouldn't come back now — would he?

Right, first things first: try the door.

Tentatively she pushed against where she thought the latch was. Nothing budged. She tried again, harder. Nothing.

Again, this time with the strength of her shoulder against the wood.

Still nothing!

Briefly she wondered how long it would take for her to die through lack of oxygen, how often she'd ever seen the caretaker mop or polish the floor, and whether anyone would miss her if she died in here with only a smelly mop for company.

Then she told herself to get a grip and managed to grope in her backpack, which had somehow on her speedy retreat into the cupboard managed to remain the right way up. At last her fingers stroked the edge of a plastic store card, of which she had many and varied. Ah! She felt for the short side and inserted it into the gap where the doors met in the middle, then slid the card up until it hit the bottom of the latch.

Good. Placing her finger there to mark the spot, she pulled the card out then slid it back in again level with where she thought the latch should be.

Sure enough it met resistance. Hoping the plastic wouldn't buckle, she pushed harder and was rewarded with a satisfying click. Thank God for an old-fashioned nineteen-thirties latch.

A welcome rush of air greeted her as she tumbled out of the cupboard. She felt she never wanted to see or smell a floor mop again for as long as she lived.

The stairway looked just as it always did: utterly soulless. It was deserted, showing no evidence that anyone apart from Laurie lived there. Half unable to believe what had just happened, Laurie shakily climbed the stairs back to her landing. Her flat door was shut. She lifted the front door mat, with its design of three bay trees, with her toe. The spare key was missing. Gingerly, she inserted her usual key in the lock of the door and making as little noise as possible, slowly turned it.

She pushed the door open. The tiny hall was undisturbed. She shook her head as though to clear it. If it hadn't been for the absence of the spare front door key under the mat she would have thought she'd imagined the last five minutes. She took a couple of steps to the living room and stood in the doorway. Somehow she'd expected chaos, but it didn't look as though the place had been ransacked. Her home looked normal, or almost normal. Her eyes alighted on the open doors of the cabinet and then the unfamiliar khaki travel bag pushed in the gap between the sofa and the wall.

So Gemma had made it after all. That at least explained the missing spare key.

'Gemma,' she called hesitantly. 'Are you here?'

Uncertainly, she carried on past the half-dead pot plant which rested on the cabinet with its open doors, through the sitting room towards the bedroom and bathroom which led off. As far as she could see nothing was missing.

'Hello,' she called again.

Silence, apart from the hoot of a passing car.

A shiver ran through her. How many times had she watched this scenario before on the TV? But this was different. This was her, Laurie, not some actress with huge frightened eyes and an annoying habit of screeching. Besides, it was perfectly light; there was no howling wind or crashing thunder. It was her, Laurie Kendal, in broad daylight, in her own home. The idea that anything could be amiss was absurd.

Squaring her shoulders, Laurie pushed on through to the bedroom and felt goosebumps on her arms. Her bedside lamp was on the floor — that was the first thing she noticed, followed by the fact that the always dodgy curtain rail was now skewed halfway off the wall with the curtain hanging drunkenly to one side.

Laurie's eyes widened.

Protruding from the end of the other side of the bed was a foot encased in a canvas boot.

She'd seen that boot before.

'Oh God.' Hardly daring to look, Laurie took another small step at the foot of the bed, peered over the edge, and then gasped in horror.

It was Gemma, and she looked very dead.

*　*　*

What to do? What to do?

Laurie stared down at Gemma's sprawled body, then after nerving herself up for it, she knelt on the rug beside her and felt an outstretched arm for a pulse. No pulse. Nerving herself still further, she brushed a reddish-blond curl from the side of Gemma's neck, her fingers and eyes searching for any sign of movement denoting life. No discernible pulse there either.

Right, call the police.

With a last look at the face of her one-time friend, Laura shakily got to her feet and picked up her rucksack from where she'd dropped it at the bedroom door. Furiously she pushed buttons. Wouldn't you just know it? Her mobile was dead. Battery showing empty.

She stared at the phone long and hard, as if by doing so she could bring it to life again. She'd started to shake now and her teeth were chattering. For a moment all she wanted to do was scream just like the feeble heroines on the box when they found a dead body unexpectedly. Perhaps they weren't so feeble after all.

What was she thinking? She was here, alone with a dead body! This was real. She needed to get out of here — and fast. Barely stopping to seize her rucksack or to close the flat door, Laurie managed to get to the head of the stairs and cling onto the rail. She looked round at the deserted landing.

Last Saturday Kathy, the librarian lady who lived in the next-door flat, had asked Laurie to feed her pet fish while she was away for a week. 'Only a pinch. Every day is best of course, but it won't matter if you miss a day.' And as instructed Laurie had obeyed instructions — *see, Mum, I can be responsible* — and had indeed performed her chore that very morning.

So, no Kathy. The only other two flats on her landing looked very empty, as they usually did at this time of day. No help there then. And that was what she needed — help. Help, help, help! She repeated it to herself all the way down the stairs and into the street.

Outside everything looked normal. Everything *was* normal. Red buses lumbering along the busy, sunny street; tourists who had probably lost their way to be in this part of town; mothers with push chairs; businessmen walking fast with no time for dead bodies. Wildly, Laurie looked round. Where was a policeman when you wanted one?

Where was there a police station anyway?

Then she remembered. Just two streets away there was a long, low, forbidding-looking building, and it was a police station. Surely it was a police station. It couldn't possibly be a library, could it?

A picture of poor Gemma's pale, still face came into her mind and she started to run.

She'd jogged the first hundred yards before she realised that people were starting to look at her as though she was a mad woman escaped from somewhere not very pleasant, so she slowed down. It would be no earthly use going in to report a crime in this sort of state. She needed to be calm, logical, clear about the events that had taken place, or they would surely think she was a raving lunatic and have her locked up in no time.

Her mouth was dry when she reached the police station, but she managed to walk in quite calmly and wait patiently while the old man in front of her made a complaint at the desk about children, or 'little devils' as he called them, playing football on his front grass and up against his garage wall. At last, after what felt like half an hour but was probably only five minutes, the duty officer turned to her.

'Yes?'

Good, finally it was her turn.

'I thought you might be a library,' said Laurie, whose mind had suddenly gone blank.

'No, we're a police station,' said the duty officer in a tired voice. 'I'm Police Constable Peters and this is definitely a police station.'

'Yes. Right. Thank goodness.' Laurie smiled, wondering how much more unreal this could get. 'My name's Laurie Kendal. And — '

'Hold on, I'll just make a note.' Helplessly she watched as her name was written down. At last he looked up. 'What can we do for you?'

'I've come to report a body,' she went on, striving for calm.

The duty officer gave her a long, blank look. 'A body, you say?'

'Yes,' said Laurie. 'My friend . . . well she's not really my friend as in *best* friend . . . I met her in Jo'burg, you see, because I had a row with my boyfriend and she put me up and she was really good to me, so I said well, any time you're in London . . . Well, you know . . . Anyway I never thought she would, but then she did, and now she's here, but she's dead . . . ' Laurie's voice petered out miserably.

'Right,' said the duty officer, looking as though in fact things were far from right. 'And where is this body you've found, exactly?'

'In my flat,' said Laurie. 'I know who did it. Well, I don't really know; you see I don't *know* him. Never seen him before. But he has a tattoo on his neck. It's of a snake and a crocodile fighting, which is strange because I never would have thought crocodiles and snakes would fight, really. But then I don't know that much about snakes — ' Her voice slowed down. ' — or crocodiles for that matter . . . '

Constable Peters was still staring at her enquiringly and patiently.

'You don't believe me, do you?'

'Just give me a few more details. How long ago did you find this, um, body?'

'She's definitely dead. She wasn't breathing; there was no pulse. Oh my God, I think I might be going to be sick . . . ' Laurie lent against the counter. 'I'm sorry. I'm sorry. I'm trying to be calm, really I am.' She tried to smile again at Constable Peters, who had stepped backwards to a doorway and called out for someone called 'Morgan' to come there pronto.

Laurie sighed and gracefully sank to the floor as a suddenly welcome blackness descended.

2

'Drink this. It'll help.'

Laurie came round to find a plastic cup thrust under her nose by an attractive lady policeman — or make that police*woman*, Laurie thought hectically — who was squatting on the floor beside her, supporting her back and shoulders.

'If you think you lost consciousness,' said the police lady as though she was speaking to a deaf person, 'we'll have to call an ambulance and fill in all sorts of forms. Do you understand?'

Laurie understood all right, and the last thing she wanted was a visit to A&E. 'No, no, I just felt a bit woozy,' she said through teeth that felt like rubber.

'OK then, let's get you to your feet and onto a chair . . . That's right. Now, put your head between your knees for a bit. Good, well done.'

Laurie decided she quite liked the police lady, but wow, she still felt as though her spine was made of jelly. By now she'd given up on not being feeble and could hear herself groaning as she held her head in her hands.

'Now,' said the policewoman, who Laurie had figured out must be Morgan, 'when you're feeling a little better, just come through with me. We'll get you some tea and you can tell me all about it.'

'What's the problem?' A new voice had come on the scene. From Laurie's position all she could see were the bottoms of some navy trousers and a pair of boring-looking shoes. Whoever he was, he was no fashion icon.

'Name's Laura Kendal. Says she's found a body,' said Duty Officer Peters. 'Sounds a bit confused.'

'Laurie,' corrected Laurie in a weak voice.

'She needs a cup of tea,' said policewoman Morgan persistently.

'OK,' said Boring Shoes. 'I'll see her when she's ready. Perhaps you'll sit in with us, Constable Morgan.'

'No,' said Laurie more forcefully. 'You've got to do something now! He's getting away. Well, he's already gone, of course he has, but he's getting away further.' Why didn't these people understand? She lifted her head and looked up into eyes of such intensity that her breath caught in her throat.

'And who exactly is that?' asked Boring Shoes, who was also the owner of a pair of extremely blue eyes which, fringed with dark lashes as they were, appeared more astonishing than ever.

'Sn-snake-tattoo,' said Laurie once she'd got over the owner of such boring shoes possessing the most un-boring eyes she'd ever seen in her life. 'He was in my flat when I got home. I-I think he must have killed Gemma.'

'Well, if Snake-tattoo's gone and Gemma's dead, there's not much we can do for the moment . . . One thing's for sure, a dead body can't go far. Best

31

you have your cup of tea and we go through it slowly and calmly, then we'll go to your flat and see what can be done.'

'Right,' said Laurie, because it seemed the easiest thing to do.

* * *

Typical, thought Tom as he watched her sip her tea. Typical that this beautiful, wild child would turn up with a highly improbable tale, just as he was about to take his much-deserved leave. Not that he wouldn't have wanted her to turn up, because she was quite some looker, just ... why did she have to be reporting a dead body; and why now, two hours before his clocking off time?

He knew the block of flats where she lived. It was a thirties build and normally the owner-occupiers kept a low profile and out of trouble. All the same, he wouldn't have expected that Laurie would choose to live there. She had an arty look about her. Not the unkempt, living-on-the-edge sort of arty; more the cultured but eccentric type. Her thick hair was the colour of dried-out grass, but much darker at the roots, and was held up at the crown with an unusual wooden clasp. The eyes that had first stared up at him from under straight eyebrows were an interesting tawny brown. She looked scared, but under control, although the lips of her generous mouth had trembled slightly when she'd said 'Snake-tattoo' in one of those quietly confident voices that smacked of a good education and most of life's privileges.

Not that she'd made that much of an impression, he told himself. It was just that it was part of his job to notice people. He'd observed, for instance, that she had a small mole to the left-hand side of her luscious lips, and that one of her front teeth slightly overlapped the other in a way that made her seem rather vulnerable. He would put her at about five foot six, with long legs and a shortish body that curved in all the right places. Not made up, clear skin too. Oh, and small, ladylike hands and feet.

No, she hadn't made a huge impression. Why should she?

Her clothes, consisting of a crumpled linen skirt and top, were nondescript, and the black canvas rucksack on the floor next to her chair was one of thousands bought the world over. He turned his attention to her printed leather sandals, which he'd recognised as 'good' immediately; good but battered. She didn't seem to care too much about appearances then.

At this point he became aware that he was staring at the wild child perhaps more than was necessary and that both Peters and Morgan had noticed this. 'OK,' he said wanting to please her in some way at the same time as sounding decisive, 'I suggest we return to your flat.'

'We should have gone before,' said the woman, scraping her chair back and getting to her feet. 'Straight away

. . . We've been wasting time. Thank you for the tea, but it really wasn't necessary. We need to find the guy who killed Gemma.'

Tom sighed wearily. 'Do you know how many crackpot reports we receive a week?' he asked in what he thought was a reasonable tone.

The wild child's remarkable tawny eyes narrowed. 'Are you saying I'm a crackpot?' she asked coldly.

So much for trying to please her.

'We had a girl in here two weeks ago, weeping all over the place saying her boyfriend had attacked her with a knife. Turned out he'd *happened* to have a knife in his hand; he was cutting a roll in half at the time and all he'd done was turn round to make a point with the knife still in his hand. That was it — end of story. Another time we had a guy in here who reported seeing a murder. Turned out he was writing a book and wanted to authenticate police procedure.'

'What's that got to do with me? I'm

not writing a book. All I'm asking is for you to take me seriously and come and see Gemma's body.'

'And we are. We are!' Tom tried not to get angry; there was something about this girl that was getting under his skin and he didn't like it. 'There's a patrol car outside. DC Morgan and I will come back to your flat with you right now.' He set his mouth in a grim line. Who did she think she was to tell him his job?

The building was the one he'd thought it might be. They went through the small vestibule. Nothing untoward there. He took the lead going up the stairs and at the top glanced round the small landing. Again, nothing.

He noticed the girl's fingers shaking as she carefully fitted her key in the lock before turning it. She stood back to let them enter first. Slowly the three of them took the two paces that constituted the tiny hall and entered the living room. There was a sofa and a couple of easy chairs. The TV was pushed against one wall and a laptop was resting on a side table next to a cabinet sporting a half-dead aloe vera plant. There were a couple of doors open in the cabinet revealing a stack of DVDs, some papers, and a bundle of what looked like knitting. Tom blinked. Somehow he couldn't imagine the wild child as being the knitting type.

'Anything missing here?' asked Morgan.

'Not as far as I can tell,' said the girl. 'Once I found Gemma, I didn't stop to look.'

Tom raised his eyebrows in her direction. 'Through here?'

She nodded, her eyes suddenly looking fearful.

Tom went through to the bedroom. After a minute he came out again. 'OK, you've had your fun,' he said in a voice that was close to seething.

'What d'you mean?' She pushed past Morgan into the bedroom and stared intently at the gap between the bed and the window. All she saw was an expanse of empty carpet. No Gemma — dead or otherwise.

'I don't understand it,' she said. She

felt slightly sick, as though this couldn't possibly be happening to her. 'She was here. I saw her . . . And where's my rug gone? There was a rug here. It was patterned — I never did like it — but it's gone. And the curtain rail had been knocked skew-whiff. That's been put back, too . . . I don't understand it.' She looked from one to the other of them. 'Am I going mad?'

Morgan cleared her throat politely and exchanged a knowing glance with Tom.

'Well, let's hope not,' Tom said in a voice devoid of emotion. 'You are, however, wasting police time.'

'You think I'm lying?' Her eyes widened. 'Why would I?'

Tom shrugged. 'People do.'

'Well not *this* people — I mean person. I'm not lying.'

There was an uncomfortable pause. The tawny eyes blinked rapidly and for a moment Tom had to resist the very unpolicemanly urge to put an arm round her shoulders.

'OK, Laura, take it steady,' said Morgan. 'Tell us again what happened.'

Laurie took a deep breath. 'First,' she said, 'my name is Laurie, OK?' For some reason it seemed important to get that right. Then she re-enacted as far as possible exactly what had happened, repeating as accurately as she could recall what she had overheard. She even went so far as to take them down the stairs and explain about her dive into the cupboard.

'Why didn't you phone us?' asked Morgan while the policeman, who Laurie had discovered was called DI Jessop, inspected the cupboard.

'I tried to, but my phone was dead — battery ran out.'

'You said the latch clicked? How did you get out then?' asked DI Jessop, eyeing the cupboard as though he didn't believe she'd ever been in there in the first place.

Wordlessly, Laurie fished in her rucksack for her store card and demonstrated how from within the

39

cupboard she'd managed to push the latch back and escape.

'Resourceful, aren't you, Laura?' DI Jessop said.

'My name's *Laurie*, not Laura.' DI Jessop laughed. 'What's so amusing?'

'Nothing, really. Just wondering why anyone would name their daughter after a motor vehicle.'

Policewoman Morgan sniggered, and Laurie decided she didn't like her very much after all.

'It was after a character in a Rodgers and Hammerstein musical, actually. Spelled L-A-U-R-I-E. Although what it's got to do with you, I can't think.'

'Well, seems like you inherited your parents' love of amateur dramatics anyway,' said DC Morgan with another snigger.

Laurie suddenly felt angry. 'Look, I don't know why you're being so obstructive — '

'Let's go back to your flat,' said DC Morgan. 'Check again and see if anything's missing.'

With a swish of her hair, Laurie went upstairs ahead of them and barged her way straight through to the bedroom. She was beginning to feel angry. The curtain rod was back in place, although she knew that if she jerked it with too much force it would fall off the wall again in the way it always had. The lamp was once more in its place on the bedside table. She leaned over and opened the drawer. Her jewellery, such as it was, lay beneath her scarves. She could see at a glance that her only valuable pieces were amongst the untidy mismatched heap of fake and real gold and silver.

Slowly, she turned to see that the police officers were behind her. 'No, nothing's missing, apart from the rug,' she admitted. 'But he said he'd got whatever it was he was looking for . . . '

With a half-smile DI Jessop sighed and turned away. 'And, only a little thing, but where's the body? No body, no crime. And you said yourself — nothing's missing.'

This really wasn't going to plan. Laurie looked round wildly. 'But my rug's missing. I told you that . . . Gemma could have been wrapped in it and taken away. That's what must have happened.' She looked from one disbelieving face to the other and heard her voice rising. 'It's the only explanation!'

'Look, just calm down . . . ' said DI Jessop.

'I am calm! Look, it's not every day you find a body in your flat.'

There was a short silence. The absence of a body was all too obvious.

DI Jessop took a small step back. 'Maybe you watched a film last night and your imagination got the better of you,' he said gently.

Suddenly, she really was getting angry. 'Don't patronise me!'

Policewoman Morgan coughed. 'We could quite easily charge you with wasting police time, you know,' she said in a voice that Laurie was sure she thought was patient and understanding. The sort of voice people used when talking to someone who wasn't quite all there.

Laurie drew herself up to her full height. 'Or you could take me seriously and do something about it.'

Now it was DI Jessop's turn again. What was this — good cop, bad cop? 'Well what do you suggest we do?'

Determined that they would not intimidate her, Laurie pushed her hair from her forehead and stood her ground. 'I don't know,' she said. 'Who's the policeman round here? You are, not me, right? As I said before, take some fingerprints or something.'

DI Jessop sighed. 'Have you any idea how much a forensic team costs?'

'So, a missing person counts for nothing?'

'You don't know she's missing. There's no blood . . . no body. How would you say this hypothetical person was killed? Knife wound? No blood. Gun shot? Ditto. Strangulation? You said she just looked as though she was asleep . . . Strange sort of dead body.'

Laurie swallowed. Suddenly, she could

43

see how implausible the whole thing sounded.

DI Jessop was staring at her penetratingly out of his intense blue eyes. 'Tell you what — perhaps you saw what you thought was a dead body. Perhaps she *was* asleep. Perhaps she woke up, you weren't here, she decided she couldn't wait and even now she's sitting on a train on her way to see her relatives. You'll probably get a phone call soon, telling you just that.'

'She was dead,' said Laurie stubbornly. 'I felt for a pulse.'

'They can be difficult to find . . . Anyone can make a mistake.'

'What about Snake-tattoo?'

PC Morgan used her fingers to tick off points. 'No proper name. Never seen him before. No evidence he's ever been here. Nothing missing.'

There was a longer silence this time, during which Laurie saw the two police officers exchange knowing glances again.

'Have you checked your phone?' asked DC Morgan eventually.

'I-I told you, it needs charging,' said Laurie hesitantly.

'There you are then,' said DC Morgan in that same hatefully placatory voice. 'Obviously your friend couldn't get through to you even if she wanted to. You need to charge your phone, get a decent night's sleep and phone this Gemma in the morning . . . If you have more cause for alarm, we'll look into it further. But I have to tell you, we can't consider a twenty-seven-year-old woman as being missing after only an hour. It's totally unrealistic.'

Laurie looked from face to face. The expressions on them told her they thought she was at best misguided, and at worst completely barking.

She only registered that they were actually leaving when DI Jessop looked over his shoulder and said, 'You should get some rest. You seem overwrought.'

Overwrought?

As though she were a zombie, she moved to close the front door behind them. They were halfway down the

45

stairs by now but their voices floated up the stairwell.

'What d'you think?' came DI Jessop's voice.

'Nutcase,' replied PC Morgan with a short laugh.

Laurie shut the door. Shakily she went to her tiny kitchen and put the kettle on. Somehow the thought of a glass of wine no longer appealed.

DC Morgan was right. She was going mad. That was it. Totally and completely doolally. Then, remembering clearly her first glimpse of a canvas-booted foot jutting out at the end of the bed; remembering Gemma's head positioned at an odd angle, her pale face, her reddish frizzy hair spread out on the rug like a fan, she closed her eyes and put a hand to her head.

The vividness of the scene came back to her full force. Real? Of course it had been real. And the police hadn't even bothered to take fingerprints! How could she have let herself be fobbed off so easily?

What had Snake-tattoo said? Something about needing a clean-up job? Well, they'd certainly done a clean-up job. So cleaned up, no one believed her and she'd even come close to disbelieving herself.

Still feeling angry at not being taken seriously, she poured out a mug of tea and took it into the living room. She'd left the doors on the cabinet open, and she wasn't going to touch them either, just in case the blue-eyed policeman and his sidekick changed their minds about the fingerprints. Then just as suddenly as it had come, the anger left her and, feeling incredibly tired, she leaned against the back of the sofa, letting her eyes wander and her mind drift. The living room was sparsely furnished; it didn't take long for her scan to take in the whole of its contents. Wearily, she glanced down to pick up her mug. Then, as her eye alighted on the khaki holdall, she sat up so fast that some of the hot liquid spilled onto her skirt.

Idiot! Here was proof! Gemma's bag, of course. Why had she forgotten it?

It had been neatly stowed between the sofa arm and the wall, not intrusive in any way; and somehow, after finding Gemma's body, all other discrepancies had been forgotten.

Now she had a dilemma. Should she open it, or make the trip back to the police station, this time dragging a full-to-bursting holdall with her?

It was a no-brainer. Hardly stopping to balance her mug rather precariously on the arm of the sofa, she ran back into the kitchen, dabbed ineffectively at her skirt, then took some rubber gloves from under the sink. *That was clever, Laurie*, she commended herself. There would be no crime scene contamination to be laid at her door. Certainly not.

There was a silly little combination lock on the zip and immediately Laurie knew exactly what the combination would be. Gemma had had a birthday while she was staying with her and she'd told her then that she used her birth year backwards for everything. *'I'm two years older than you,'* she remembered Gemma saying with a laugh. *'But don't tell anyone, will you? I always lie about my age. That way nobody can ever guess my pin number or combination codes or anything. Not that I pack anything remotely valuable in my baggage. Anything worth taking is always in my hand luggage and I don't let that out of my sight.'*

Surely though, there must be something of interest in her baggage. But, ten minutes later, Laurie sat back on her heels with a defeated expression on her face. Thank goodness she hadn't contacted DI Jessop again before opening the bag, because its contents proved nothing. All it consisted of was dirty washing and a paperback novel, all of which Laurie recognised could equally well have belonged to any girl of a similar age to Gemma, or even to herself for that matter.

So, where did that leave her? She knew now that Gemma had certainly been here, but who else would believe her? It seemed likely that Gemma had been mixed up in some sort of illegal activity in Johannesburg. She was in trouble and had to run, and that had been behind her sudden visit to London. Somewhere at the periphery of her brain, Laurie registered that she was unsurprised in coming to this conclusion. She tried to think with Gemma's mind which, it now transpired, she knew less well than she'd thought. So things had got too hot for her in Jo'burg, she'd decided to lose herself in London until things calmed down, but she'd been followed . . .

Wait a minute — that didn't make any kind of sense. Snake-tattoo had said he'd been disturbed, and he thought it had been by the owner of the flat — Laurie. He'd used her name — well, 'Laura'. So, why had he been in her flat in the first place? And how did he know that someone called Laura or Laurie owned it? She dismissed now the idea that Snake-tattoo was a common or garden-variety burglar. What sort of burglar would walk past a laptop and leave jewellery nestling in the top drawer of the bedside table, undisturbed? No, Snake-tattoo had come here in order to take something specific. The only coincidence was that he'd come on the same day Gemma had arrived — and then what? Just killed her because she was there?

A bit extreme wasn't it? A bit too coincidental?

And what had he been looking for? It wasn't as though Laurie had anything remotely valuable. The most valuable thing she possessed was the flat itself, and that was only because her dad had helped her with the deposit. She wouldn't have even been here if she hadn't fallen out with her boyfriend, who was probably still in Jo'burg right now. Or maybe he'd moved on to some other exotic location and was photographing stick-thin models dressed in skimpy clothes, even as Laurie sat here puzzling as to how on earth a dead body could first appear, then with equal speed disappear, from her flat.

Laurie winced. No, now was not the time to be thinking about boyfriends, especially ex-boyfriends.

The thing was, remembering Snake-tattoo's phone conversation, he seemed to think he'd got hold of whatever it was he'd been looking for. 'Found it!' he'd said. Or words to that effect. Well, he hadn't been carrying anything other than his rucksack, so whatever it was had to be small enough to be carried in there.

Hold on! Laurie backtracked a bit. Hold on a minute! Hand baggage? OK, so the khaki holdall contained Gemma's washing, clothes etcetera, but what about her personal things? Her purse, her passport, her makeup? Her phone?

Where were they? Where was her rucksack? The one that was a sister to Laurie's own rucksack, that was even now sitting on the sofa next to her. Black canvas, cheap, serviceable; just the job both for travelling and everyday use at home. Gemma and she had bought them in a sale together.

So, where was Gemma's?

For a moment Laurie felt herself back into the smelly cupboard, looking through the crack. Snake tattoo with a black canvas rucksack on his shoulder.

It had to be Gemma's.

But why would he want Gemma's rucksack? He was in Laurie's flat. He knew he was in Laurie's flat. He thought he'd killed Laurie. Laurie had no reason to believe he'd even heard of Gemma.

But the fact remained, it seemed Snake-tattoo had taken Gemma's rucksack. Perhaps he'd taken it as part of the clear-up job and put whatever else he'd found that he'd wanted inside it.

It was a puzzle. What could she have that anyone else could possibly want? Laurie went to take another sip of her by now stone-cold, tea then suddenly froze with the mug halfway to her lips.

Suppose he'd thought the rucksack

belonged to Laurie? Well, he must have thought it was Laurie's, if he didn't even know about Gemma — right? Sooner or later Snake-tattoo would open the rucksack, and when he did he'd realise his mistake — that the rucksack belonged to a girl called Gemma, not Laurie at all. He'd realise he had the wrong rucksack, therefore the wrong girl. Then, surely, he'd be back to rectify his mistake.

Laurie's eyes widened with horror. And here she was, sitting on the sofa drinking tea! What to do? *Think Laurie, think!*

But maybe he wouldn't. Maybe he had found the thing he was looking for and just stuck it in the rucksack for expediency's sake. Why should he care whose rucksack he had? And killing Laurie hadn't been the main object of the exercise after all. Couldn't have been. That just didn't bear thinking about.

Even so, she didn't feel very safe. Suppose he did come back? Entirely uninvited, a picture of Gemma's pale, lifeless face flashed before her eyes. He'd had no compunction in killing once . . .

One good thing was that he had no idea what Laurie looked like. Couldn't have, or he wouldn't have mistaken Gemma for her. Perhaps, having got what he wanted, he'd just dump Gemma's rucksack and not bother coming back.

But there was still the 'what if'.

Her teeth were chattering by now. She was still seriously scared.

One thing was clear: she'd have to get out. No use staying here like a sitting duck.

Laurie jumped to her feet, went through to the bedroom and pulled her own holdall, which was black with a green patterned strap, from her ward-robe. Five minutes later she'd packed spare jeans, T-shirts, sweaters and enough underclothes to last her a few days. Was she being hysterical to take her passport and laptop as well?

Where on earth could she go?

But she wasn't thinking about that right now. The important thing was to get out. After that she could phone her mum and dad up in north Essex, maybe stay with them for a few days. Thinking of this, she pulled a face. She could imagine already the knowing looks they'd exchange. Laurie the wayward again. What sort of muddle had she got into this time?

Just in time she remembered to stop and pick up her phone charger from the kitchen. As she did so she caught sight of the sign she'd stuck on the fridge — *don't forget to feed the fish*.

The fish! What would she do about next door's fish?

Oh, for goodness sake, they were only fish. Surely they could last a few days. She'd give them extra tonight.

Eventually she was ready. She hoisted her rucksack over her shoulder and let herself out of the flat. The sooner she was out of the building the better.

At the top of the stairs she stopped.

Suppose the building was being watched? Suppose Snake-tattoo and his cronies had opened the rucksack and had accessed Gemma's phone? Suppose there was a photo of Laurie on her phone?

With unwelcome clarity, Laurie recalled Gemma pointing her phone at her at the airport not once, but several times. The photos could still be on there. And if it *was* Laurie they were after . . .

Even now, Snake-tattoo, realising his mistake, could be watching, waiting for night to fall before breaking in again to rectify it. He wouldn't even have to break in, for heaven's sake; he already had the spare key!

Was she being hysterical?

The icy sweat that began to form on Laurie's spine told her that even if she was, she should act on her instincts. She shouldn't take chances. Self-preservation was the name of the game.

She couldn't go out the front way, that was for sure. But the back entrance led out into a small car park where those residents who were lucky enough to own a car parked their vehicles. It was deserted and poorly lit at night. Maybe she'd be safer going down the front steps as she'd first intended, choosing a busy time like now, when she could mingle with the rush-hour crowds and disappear on the Underground. After all, she had a very good working knowledge of it.

Then, remembering the fish again, she smacked her hand to her forehead.

She had the answer right here in her rucksack. The key to the flat next door. The *empty* flat next door.

For the first time in what felt like a lifetime, Laurie's lips curved into a smile. After a last look round, she vacated her own flat and headed purposefully for the one next door.

★　★　★

Tom felt uneasy.

He wasn't quite sure why that should be, because everything at the office was up to date and he should have been quite happy to get away and start preparing for his much-looked-forward-to cycling holiday.

Although he was conscientious — well, as conscientious as the next man, he would have thought — he wasn't used to this strange feeling at the back of his mind that he'd forgotten to do something, or overlooked something of extreme importance. And this feeling of having failed to finish off, to tie every end, stayed with him even after he'd left the station and driven home to his purpose-built flat through half an hour of London's thickest traffic.

That he'd deliberately taken the route which took him past Laurie's block, he was only too aware, but he still didn't connect the itchy feeling at the back of his mind with her particular situation.

Quite what she'd been playing at, he had no idea. But he wasn't paid to psychoanalyse every whacky wild child he came across, even if she was attractive enough to make his heartbeat rev up a notch or two.

Suddenly, despite all his intentions to the contrary, Tom found himself remembering Laurie's tawny eyes as she'd looked up at him for the first time. He admitted to himself that actually she was more than a 'looker'; she was thought-provoking in a pretty insistent way. Why couldn't she have come in merely to report a stray cat or something similar? Then he could have just flirted with her very gently and simply watched her walk out of the station, and that would have been that. No worrying about whether or not she'd been telling the truth, and she *had* found a dead body, and it *had* disappeared. And what had he, DI Jessop, done about it? He frowned. That was easy. DI Jessop had done a big fat nothing.

But what could he have done? his saner self argued. As DC Morgan had assured him on their way back to the station, no body — no crime. All they had to go on was a crazy story delivered by a girl who had queued up calmly and patiently for five minutes and then staged a hysterical fainting fit when she thought she wasn't getting enough attention.

No, he'd done everything required of him. His conscience was clear.

But still, when he passed the block of flats where Laurie lived he was relieved to see it wasn't on fire; there was no ambulance drawn up outside, or even a gang of hooded youths hanging about outside looking for trouble. So, no reason to slow down his car as he went past hoping for a glimpse of her; no reason to even glance over towards Laurie's bedroom window before speeding the car up again in order to keep up with the traffic. But to his annoyance, he'd still done so.

He'd feel differently about it tomorrow, he was sure he would. But if he still had a niggle at the back of his brain, perhaps he'd come by this way in the morning and have a hearty breakfast at the café across the road. It was a good café; he'd eaten there before. He always had a good breakfast before a bike ride anyway, and it wouldn't be far out of his way.

He gave a half smile.

To him, it all made perfect sense.

3

Laurie had spent a fitful night on her librarian neighbour's bed. Her finer feelings had prevented her from actually getting between the sheets. It would be shocking enough for Kathy to come home and discover that her pet fish had died of starvation, without finding that her whacky next-door neighbour had also had a Goldilocks moment in her absence. She had, however, taken the liberty of plugging her phone charger into a kitchen socket. A couple of folded throws were neatly stacked on the blanket box at the foot of the bed, so after double-locking the front door she took them to use as blankets.

Then with a weary sigh, she'd crawled into her makeshift bed and considered her options for the next day.

If, as seemed likely — after all, he'd clearly said 'got it' — Snake-tattoo had found what he wanted and put it in the rucksack he believed belonged to Laurie, why would he come back? Why would he even bother to examine the rucksack's contents? If he hadn't been disturbed he probably would have emptied its contents and left them behind anyway; wouldn't even bother with the phone or any other stuff. If he'd only needed the rucksack as a means of transport so to speak, he could just throw the whole lot away, once he'd retrieved whatever it was he wanted.

She pondered, for maybe the millionth time, on whatever this object of desirability was that Snake-tattoo sought so desperately. As usual her mind remained blank.

But obviously it had been very important. Important enough to kill for. Realising all over again that she couldn't take chances, she gave an involuntary shudder. The sensible thing to do was to stay away from the vicinity for the immediate future. Well, a few days at least.

She'd already informed the agency she worked for that she had a friend coming and was taking the remainder of the week off. So, there was nothing to stop her from jumping on the train in the morning and visiting her parents. They'd be annoyed, of course they would, that she'd somehow managed to get herself into yet another pickle; but they'd help her, naturally — she was their daughter, after all.

Trying not to cringe, she pictured their expressions as she attempted to explain. Her mother's patient but resigned eyes; her father baffled and disappointed as he turned away. *Not again* hanging unspoken in the air between them.

Perhaps she wouldn't have to tell them after all. Perhaps after a good night's sleep, she'd think of a way round it.

Eventually, despite all the crazy stuff whirling round in her brain making her head feel like a food processor, she drifted into a semi-conscious state and slept as best she could between dreams of crocodiles and policemen with extraordinarily blue eyes, taking it in turn to chase her through the Underground.

After tossing and turning for what felt like most of the night, she was relieved on fully waking to discover that both her watch and stomach were telling her it was nearly breakfast time. Well, she was still alive! She'd slept so fitfully that she was almost certain that no one had visited her flat in the night. Surely the slightest creak from next door would have had her wide awake.

Cautiously she peered out of the window. Although she was viewing it from a slightly different angle than from that of her own flat, the street appeared to be as usual. There were no suspicious-looking characters lurking in shop doorways and no sign of Snake-tattoo loitering by the news-stand on the corner. Everything looked normal. Laurie gave a small sigh of relief.

Of course, she knew she'd been

overreacting. Last night she'd allowed her imagination to run away with her. Stupid, really. Now she'd spent an unnecessarily uncomfortable night, when she could have been fast asleep tucked up in her own bed.

But she'd still ring home and somehow, without worrying her mum and dad, wangle an invitation to spend a few days in north Essex with them. Yes, even though she wasn't as anxious as before, she was still convinced that spending time away from London might be a wise option. If the opportunity arose she might even confide in her parents. They might even believe her!

After cleaning her teeth and having a sketchy wash, she read the instructions on the fish food and decided that as today was Thursday and Kathy was due home on Saturday, Sonny and Cher, the fish, should survive for long enough. Briefly, she wondered whether leaving a note would be in order. Then, as the thought of putting the events of the last twenty-four hours into words that made any form of coherence overwhelmed her, she decided best not. What the librarian's eye didn't see, her heart wouldn't grieve over.

Her newly charged phone showed only one missed message from yesterday. It was from Gemma; brief and to the point. *Arrived UK. CUL8R.* She'd probably been on the Underground when that came through. Nothing since. Not a lot to learn from that then.

Her stomach growled, reminding her that she hadn't eaten since a sandwich at tea break yesterday morning. No wonder she couldn't think straight. She'd go to the café over the road and have a decent breakfast before phoning her mum.

Laurie peeked out of the window again. Everything looked clear. As silently as possible, she let herself out of Kathy's flat and pocketed the key. Then, holding her breath, she listened carefully outside her own front door before inserting her key in the lock and quietly opening it. The flat was as she'd left it: Gemma's holdall still wedged between the sofa arm and the wall, cabinet doors still half open, the rest of the sparsely furnished rooms all exactly as they'd been left by whoever had done the 'clear-up' job.

Slowly Laurie let out her breath. No, the whole thing had not just been a bad dream. Even if the phone message hadn't already told her, the half-opened cabinet doors and Gemma's holdall did now.

She backed out onto the landing and quietly went down the stairs. From just inside the swing doors she glanced as far up and down the street as she could, before confidently walking out of the building and straight across to the café.

It was still only just after seven thirty; the café had not long opened. Pilar, the plump, genial Italian lady who ran the place, looked up and gave a surprised smile when she recognised Laurie.

'Early bird today?' she queried.

'Right,' said Laurie, plonking down her holdall and taking her rucksack from her shoulder. 'Got a train to catch. Can I just have a mug of tea to be going on with? And I'd like a full breakfast but with only one egg, when you've got started.'

Maria smiled. 'Sure. I bring you your tea pronto.'

'No rush,' said Laurie with a smile.

She chose a table in the front corner, facing the street, and sat down with a sigh of relief. Just being out of Burleigh Mansions made her feel better.

'Tea.' As she placed a steaming mug on the table, Maria's bulk momentarily blocked out the street view. 'Is nice day today. Just warm, not too much sun.'

'Should suit me then,' replied Laurie, who liked Pilar and happily passed the time of day with her on the occasions she popped in.

Pilar nodded at the holdall. 'You go travelling again?'

'Yes; not so far this time, and not for so long. Just to my parents' for a few days.'

'Good. Is good that you visit them.'

Although, thinking of her father, Laurie didn't quite agree with the sentiment, she nodded because it was easier. Pilar moved away, and as Laurie picked up her mug she glanced out of the window — and wished she hadn't.

There was nothing, bar the menu advertising breakfast written on the window, to impede her vision, so she had a clear view of a muscled back clad in a tight T-shirt, and a thick neck above it which ended with a shaven head, all less than a foot away from her! He seemed to be staring across the road at Burleigh Mansions, in the direction of Laurie's bedroom window.

Her mug still halfway to her lips, Laurie sat as though carved from stone, surveying the tattoo on the neck of the guy standing right outside the café window with his back to her.

If he were to turn, he'd see her!

As soon as the realisation dawned she instinctively ducked her head and put a hand up to shield her face. A minute later, when she dared to raise her eyes again, he was halfway across the road.

Dear God, she thought, *if you make him go away, I'll be good for ever and ever.*

But he didn't go away. Instead he stopped right outside the building and took a mobile phone from his pocket. Good; his attention would be taken for a moment.

Laurie moved from her table at the front of the café towards one further back. She dumped her holdall on the floor. That was better. Although she could still keep Snake-tattoo within her sights, she was pretty sure he wouldn't be able to see her clearly in the shadowy interior of the cafe.

But, before she could sit down, her mobile rang.

Stupidly she stared at her phone, and very nearly answered it. The caller was Gemma. How could that be? Gemma was dead. Then she looked across the road. Snake-tattoo had his phone to his ear and was pacing up and down outside the flats.

Now, don't panic. Don't answer it. Just ignore it. Watching him, she let her mobile ring until it clicked to answer service. No message was left.

He had opened Gemma's rucksack then; he'd found Gemma's phone and of course Laurie's number. And he'd just called it!

Why would he do that? Was he checking to see where she was? Wasn't he content that he'd killed one girl already? What on earth was this about?

'You want mushrooms?'

'Sure,' answered Laurie, thinking that actually she didn't think she could eat anything now.

'I do for you, five minutes, OK?'

'Lovely.'

Laurie took a sip of tea and watched as Snake-tattoo pocketed the mobile and, as though he had a perfect right to be there, entered the swing doors to the block of flats.

So, he was going back to her flat.

She'd stopped shaking now. All right, so she was scared. But what could he actually do while she was sat here in a café with Pilar, who knew her, could vouch for her, and would let no one take her by force?

She could ring the police, tell them he was there. Tell them she wasn't going mad and she could prove it. But picking up her phone again she hesitated. If she dialled 999, what would happen? It would take forever to get a car here, and by that time Snake-tattoo would have disappeared again and she'd be charged with wasting police time. Shame she didn't have DI Jessop's number; that would have been handy. Then she caught herself on the thought. DI Jessop? Just because he had blue eyes and an attractive smile didn't mean he'd be any more sympathetic today than he was yesterday.

Should she make a move now; forget her breakfast which actually, now she came to think of it, smelled quite delicious? She should have done that as soon as he disappeared into the building — just fled the café and disappeared into the Underground, where she felt safe. It was way too late now. He could be watching out of the flat window.

But why, she thought, why on earth would he be looking for her?

The café door opened and a couple of workmen came in. 'Two full breakfasts, love, and two teas.' One of them smiled in Laurie's direction and the two of them sat at a table opposite her. They were burly types. Good, safety in numbers. If Snake-tattoo did decide he was hungry and came in here in order to watch the flat — although why he would do so was still beyond Laurie's comprehension — she'd have a bit more backup. The two workmen wouldn't allow him to drag her off, kicking and screaming as she was sure she would be, to a destination unknown.

'Breakfast — enjoy.' Pilar placed a sizzling, hot plate in front of her.

'That looks good. Thanks.' Goodness, she was hungry after all. The bacon smelt divine and she was sure to feel better when she'd eaten. Hardly taking her eyes from the street, Laurie cut up her food and prepared to relish her breakfast as much as was possible with one eye still firmly on the scene outside.

She'd managed to demolish one rasher of bacon and half an egg, and was about to start on a sausage, when from the corner of her eye she saw Snake-tattoo run lightly down the steps and without a glance in the direction of the café set off down the street towards the Underground.

Great! But now what? Should she go back over to the flat to see what else was missing? Maybe he'd taken a fancy to her electric kettle this time, or one of her Ikea cushions, she thought with a relief that was fast turning to hysteria. No, stick to the plan. She'd finish her breakfast, maybe even have another cup of tea; then, at a more reasonable hour, she'd phone home and make arrangements.

The bell on the shop door went again. Uneasily, Laurie looked up.

'Oh!' she said.

'Good Lord,' said Tom.

And she seemed almost as wild this morning, he decided. There were dark circles under her eyes, which were haunted and fearful. There was a holdall next to her table and a rucksack slung over the back of her chair. Tom felt a small corner of his heart jerk uncontrollably. She looked as though she were about to embark on a journey, the thought of which scared her to death.

'Hi,' he said. 'Laurie,' he added, as an afterthought.

There was a small twitch at the corner of her lips. 'At least you managed to get my name right today.' She looked him up and down. 'You don't look as though you're on duty. Don't look plain enough for 'plain clothes'.'

Tom gave a grin; his cycling jersey was a rather bright canary yellow. He sat down in the chair opposite her. Now why had he done that? It wasn't as though he wanted a conversation with her. Although it was a relief in a way to know that she was still alive, even if she was as nutty as ever. Now at least he could go off on his holiday with a clear conscience.

'Hi Tom,' called Pilar from the counter. 'Your usual?'

'That'd be great,' answered Tom.

The tawny eyes were working over-time, studying his face intently. He watched as she frowned a little, as though deciding whether or not to be friendly. Finally she speared a piece of sausage with her fork and delicately balanced a couple of baked beans on the top. 'Never seen you in here before,' she said as she transferred the forkful to her mouth, which was as luscious as ever, Tom couldn't help noticing.

'No, I don't come in every day. Just now and then, when the mood takes me. I'm on holiday today so the mood took me.'

'Right.' She went back to her food.

'You know each other?' queried Pilar as she firmly deposited a mug of tea at Tom's elbow.

Laurie looked up. 'No,' she said at exactly the same time as Tom said 'Yes.'

'Well, not really,' he amended. 'Only a bit.'

Pilar gave them a puzzled smile, and turned her attention back to Tom. 'No black pudding today. Extra tomato OK?'

'Absolutely — thanks.' He followed Pilar with his eyes as she collected one of the workman's cups for refill on her way back to the counter.

Laurie took a sip of tea.

'I'll move to another table if you want,' said Tom.

Her eyes met his for a frightened moment. 'No, don't do that,' she said quickly.

Don't get involved, Tom, he told himself. *Think of your cycle trip.*

'Everything OK this morning?'

'No,' said Laurie shortly. 'Everything is very far from OK. It's particularly hideous — since you ask.'

Tom raised an eyebrow.

She leaned forward. 'They know,' she said in a whisper.

Oh dear, she was getting delusional again. This was what he'd been frightened of. 'Who's 'they'?'

'Whoever it is who killed Gemma, that's who . . . The crime you won't investigate, remember?'

She might be beautiful, but she really was barking. He sighed. 'No body, no crime. We went through all that yesterday.'

'You didn't believe me yesterday.'

'I don't believe you today.'

For a long moment their glances met and held. Then something totally unexpected happened. The tawny eyes suddenly filled with tears and Tom felt his heart lurch in his chest.

'Sorry.' She blinked rapidly. 'Why should you believe me? It sounds crazy even to me. Take no notice of me. I'll manage. I'll go away, stay with my parents for a few days. Perhaps when I came back they'll have forgotten about me.'

Tom had dealt with distressed females before. He'd learned from experience it was best to give them time to collect themselves.

'You never found what was missing then?' he asked after what he considered a suitable pause.

'I told you, nothing was missing.'

'Well, sometimes it takes a while for you to miss an item.'

Laurie gave a snort. 'You've seen the way I live. Minimal isn't the word. I've got most of my stuff in here.' She indicated the rucksack, kicked her holdall and gave a wry grin. 'I'm like a snail; I carry my home on my back. I'd know straight away if something had gone.'

Tom thought of the sparse interior of Laurie's flat. She was probably right.

'So what makes you think 'they' know, and what exactly is it that 'they' know?'

'They know that the rucksack they took . . . remember, I told you Snake-tattoo was carrying a rucksack like this?'

She indicated her rucksack again. 'Well, they've opened it and found it belonged to Gemma. It must have had all her personal possessions in it, passport etcetera, including her phone.'

This was going a sight too quickly for Tom. 'And how d'you know this exactly?'

Laurie leaned forward. 'Because Snake-tattoo tried to phone me on it this morning. Just now, before you came in . . . He was standing right outside this window, looking up at my bedroom. Then, he crossed the road, used his phone at exactly the same time as mine started ringing, and guess whose name came up when I went to answer it? Gemma's!'

'Enjoy.' Pilar placed his breakfast in front of him.

'Looks good. Thanks,' said Tom automatically. 'You can't know it was him,' he went on after helping himself to brown sauce. 'It could have been Gemma. She could've been ringing to tell you where she is, rucksack on her back and all.'

Laurie gave a sigh. 'It was him,' she

said. 'I thought at first it was his rucksack I saw him with — a black rucksack is common enough — but then I realised that although Gemma's holdall with her clothes and a novel are in the flat, her personal possessions weren't there and neither was her rucksack. It's just like mine; we bought them together in a sale. No way is she going to come all the way from Johannesburg with no personal possessions.'

Tom munched on his bacon, which was just a shade too crispy for his liking, just the same as the girl sitting opposite was a shade too intense. 'Look, no offence but it could still be as I said. Gemma's asleep, you find her, she doesn't know you've even been there; she wakes up, decides to leave her kit with you. Goes off with just her rucksack to visit the relatives, then this morning decides she'd better contact you and tell you what's going on. You don't answer so that's that . . . She'll probably contact you later.'

For a moment Laurie stared at him, seeming to have lost the power of speech. Tom chewed while he waited. He had the feeling she'd get it back any moment.

'And what about the fact that I found her dead . . . that's D-E-A-D — body in my flat? What about my missing rug?'

'Be reasonable. I can't send out a search party for a missing rug.' He gave a smug smile.

Laurie put her head in her hands. 'I'm too tired for this. I had to sleep on my neighbour's bed last night; she's away and I'm feeding her fish so I've got her key. I've got to get out of my flat. I don't feel safe, not even safe enough to have my breakfast there. And I was right, wasn't I? Because he came back this morning. If you'd been five minutes earlier you'd have seen him yourself! And why did he come back? Eh? Why? He's got Gemma's phone probably crammed full of photos and he's realised that the girl he killed is not Laurie Kendal. Maybe it's Laurie

Kendal he wanted all along — not Gemma. No, I'm not asking you to understand it; I don't understand it either!' She paused for breath. 'But I shouldn't have bothered you. I might have known you wouldn't listen.'

A sudden ring tone broke the silence that followed. Laurie's eyes widened as she groped in her pocket. 'Oh, it's work . . . Hello, no I haven't left yet . . . Who? . . . What? No, I don't, I've never heard of him. Listen, do me a favour. If this creep calls again don't, whatever you do, tell him I'm going to my parents' . . . Oh, you did. But not the address? Thank goodness . . . Well, thanks for telling me.'

She clicked her phone off and turned back to Tom, who was finishing his tea. 'See?' she said belligerently.

'What?' said Tom.

'Some creep has phoned the agency I work for pretending to be a friend. First off wanted to speak to me, to know where I was working this week; and when he was told I had a few days off, wanted to know where I was going. When they asked who was calling, he said he was a photographer friend of mine by the name of Mark. I don't have a photographer friend by the name of Mark.'

'Oh,' said Tom, who could think of nothing else to say.

'But the thing is, he must know I have lots of photographer friends. Well, not friends, but acquaintances. So, how did he know that? What the hell is going on?'

This was getting crazier by the second and Tom didn't like it one bit. And he was very aware he had a bike ride to be concentrating on.

'So, what are you going to do?'

'Well, I'll still go to my parents'. All that the agency told this Mark — alias Snake-tattoo, I should think — was that my parents live somewhere near Sudbury, so I should be safe once I get to them. Of course he knows what I look like now. Gemma was forever taking photos on her phone . . . Never as good on a phone of course. Not as good as my state-of-the-art Pentax. I use proper film in that, mainly black and white. I've studied photography and believe me there's a difference. But phone cameras get a reasonable likeness, don't they? Good enough to recognise someone I'd say.'

'Did you say he'd been in your flat again this morning?'

'Well, he went up the steps and inside so I reckon that's where he went, yes. He left again about five minutes later, just before you came in.'

Laurie was fiddling with her purse, obviously ready to pay her bill. Tom had finished his breakfast and his tea, although he could do with another cup really. Oh, what the hell, it would only take five minutes. 'If you like . . . ' he said, slightly surprised because suddenly he seemed to be totally out of control of his mouth and what came out of it. 'If you like, I'll come over with you and we'll check out your flat again.'

He was rewarded with a sceptical

raise of the eyebrow followed by a dazzling smile when she realised he was serious. 'Would you really?' she said. 'Would you really do that for me?'

You fool Tom, you fool!

'Be pleased to,' he said. 'And by the way, my name's Tom.'

★ ★ ★

Despite being really rather annoyed that DI Jessop or, more familiarly, Tom, still wasn't inclined to believe her fully, Laurie stepped across the street quite jauntily. It was surprising the difference it made having a policeman striding out next to her. Especially a tall, blue-eyed policeman, even if he was wearing a hideously yellow sports shirt. At least she assumed it was a sports shirt; it certainly couldn't be considered on-trend or even bucking (in a good way) the trend of fashion.

He carried her holdall all the way up to her flat too. She'd half-expected him to drop it at the bottom of the stairs, but — 'No, that's fine. It's not heavy,' he said and carried it on up as though it weighed nothing.

Laurie let them into the flat. Tom's eyes immediately searched out the khaki holdall. 'This Gemma's?'

'Yep,' said Laurie. 'You can check it if you like. But I warn you, it's full of dirty washing.'

'Does it look the same as when you left it?'

At least he was showing some curiosity, so perhaps he was starting to half-believe her.

'Yes, I think so. But he probably searched it yesterday, thinking it belonged to me. He wouldn't bother again this morning, would he?'

Tom's eyes travelled round the rest of the room. 'You've left the doors on the cabinet open.'

'Well yes, I thought you might still take fingerprints.'

'If he's as professional as you seem to think he is, there won't be any fingerprints; he'll have worn gloves.'

'Oh.'

They both went through to the bedroom. 'And you're sure nothing's missing here?'

Laurie sighed. 'When I realised that you weren't going to help me and after I'd found Gemma's holdall, I packed some stuff and went next door for the night. Oh, and I took my laptop as well and left it at Kathy's — she's the fish-loving librarian next door. My jewellery is still in my bedside table drawer. I would've noticed if anything had gone, I'm sure I would. As you can see, there's nothing of much value here, only a second-rate TV.'

'Just the same,' said Tom, 'look again. You won't have another chance if you're going away for a few days.'

With a shrug of her shoulders, Laurie opened the wardrobe and rummaged in the bottom where she kept assorted handbags and shoes, all of which were intact. She looked in the top of the wardrobe, in the gap where the holdall she'd packed last night usually sat.

'Oh my God!' She put her hand over her mouth. 'My Pentax — the camera I was telling you about. I keep it up here just by my holdall. It's gone! How could I not have noticed it was missing before?'

Tom looked unsurprised. 'It's amazing how often that happens,' he said. 'D'you think it was there yesterday when you packed your bag?'

Frowning, Laurie tried to remember pulling the holdall from the high shelf. Usually she'd take care she didn't dislodge her camera bag along with it and have it fall on her head, giving her concussion in the process. 'Yes. No! Oh, I don't know! I was so rattled and in such a hurry to get out of here . . . D'you think it might have been my camera he was after all the time? But why? It cost a lot — well, a lot to me, but not that much in the real world, I suppose . . . And to kill Gemma . . . ' Her legs suddenly felt weak and she sat down on the bed.

'OK. So let's assume it was the

camera he wanted. It's not digital, you said? So in order to look at the photos, he'd have to get the film developed. What was on the film?'

'I don't know. I had loads of stuff on there; one unfinished film in the camera and several ready to be developed, still in the bag. Stuff from when I was in Jo'burg. Probably stuff from the photo-shoot.'

'Photo-shoot?'

'Yes,' said Laurie impatiently. 'Didn't I tell you? That's the reason I went to Jo'burg in the first place. My boyfriend — well, ex-boyfriend now — is a fashion photographer. He had a long-term assignment and I went with him. After a couple of months we fell out though. We were never really right for each other anyway. I didn't really fit into his world. I was much more interested in shooting the scenery than anorexic, empty-faced models in ridiculous clothes that no one would wear in a million years; I just didn't see the point . . . Anyway, you don't want to hear all this. Thing is, I'd let my flat — this flat, and the lease didn't run out for another month, so I stayed with Gemma until I could come home again. That's why this doesn't look much like a home.' She waved her hands at her surroundings. 'I've not long been back in here again.'

'So what had you been filming while you were in Jo'burg?'

'All sorts. Hold on, why would anyone be interested in my holiday snaps?'

Tom shrugged. 'Don't know. I'm just thinking out loud. D'you develop your own?'

Laurie sighed. 'Not anymore. Used to borrow the ex-boyfriend's studio. I suppose that's why I haven't got round to developing anything yet. It's quite expensive, you know, to do it the old-fashioned way.'

'OK,' said Tom. 'I suggest you keep looking, see what else is missing.'

Randomly, Laurie opened drawers and poked in cupboards, all the time muttering to herself about not believing it, and why would anyone take her camera. She caught herself sighing and wringing her hands in the manner of a mad Lady Macbeth, and realised she'd better get a grip or Tom, who'd shown signs of at least half-believing her, would realise his mistake.

Eventually, she sat back on the bed. 'OK, I'm done,' she said.

But Tom seemed in no hurry to leave. 'What now? Will you go back to the police?'

'You are the police!'

'File a crime report at the station, I mean. You've got a missing item now.'

'Per-lease! D'you think I want a repeat of yesterday's experience? See you and DC Morgan rolling your eyes at each other? No, I'll file the claim with my insurance company later. At least there'll be a report of my visit to your station to back it up, even if I didn't find the camera to be missing immediately.'

'True,' said Tom.

Wondering if she'd been a shade ungrateful, she stole a glance at his profile as they made their way down the stairs. 'Thank you,' she said, 'for coming over with me. I know it sounded strange . . . well it *is* strange, but I feel a bit better knowing you don't think I'm lying. You don't, do you?'

Tom pushed the swing door open and held it for her to pass under his arm. As she did so her phone rang.

She glanced down at it, and felt her face pale. 'It's Gemma again,' she whispered.

4

'D'you want me to answer it?' Tom said before he could help himself.

The relief in her eyes was palpable.

Aware that he was getting in much deeper than he should, Tom took the phone from her. 'Hello,' he said. 'Who's this?'

There was a click — then silence.

'What did he say?' Laurie's eyes were wide and frightened.

'Nothing,' Tom said, looking round grimly and relieved to find that he could see no one obviously watching them. 'But right now I think we'd better move fast, just in case.'

'D'you really think we're being watched?' squeaked Laurie, running to keep up with his sudden long stride.

'Probably not, but you never know.'

There was a short silence while he guessed she was trying to take this in.

She glanced over her shoulder, then at him. 'You don't need all this,' she said after a moment. 'What about your holiday? Look, just see me to the Underground. I'll be safe then; I know my way round it like the back of my hand. It's still the morning rush hour, so it's pretty busy. No one'll spot me.'

She was trying to sound confident and almost succeeding. Now why didn't that make him feel better? Funny, he'd thought she'd jump at the idea of anyone helping her, not to mention believing her. He was oddly touched to think she didn't want to spoil his holiday.

'Where are you headed?' he asked, thinking that that would be where he was headed too.

'Liverpool Street station. Then I'll check out the trains and catch the next one to Colchester, then from there go to Sudbury either by train or bus, then on to Bury St Edmunds — that's where my parents live. I'll be fine, don't worry about me.'

'OK. We can travel together; we're heading in the same direction, at least for a bit.'

'Where are you going, then?'

Tom wished he knew. 'The idea is a bike ride taking in all the stuff I want to see along the east coast.' He gave a wry smile because the idea of this actuality ever coming to pass was becoming increasingly remote. Casually he glanced over his shoulder. There were crowds of people around but no sign of anyone answering Laurie's description of Snake-tattoo. Did he seriously think anyone was following them?

Eyes wide with an anxiety that at least she didn't put into words, Laurie quickened her step beside him. With an effort to pull himself together and treat this as a routine police matter — *young woman possibly, but probably not, being stalked by unknown person* — he smiled reassuringly. They needed to act naturally. Hoping to inspire her with confidence, he smiled again, as though they were chatting on their way like any normal travellers. 'Yep, I'd like to include a new wildlife centre at Abberton Reservoir, and some nice flat country roads in north Essex. I've got half a route planned, but it's not set in stone.'

Thinking she would probably hoot with laughter, he looked at her sideways in order to judge her reaction. Surprisingly, she only grinned. 'That sounds so good,' she said, as though putting aside for a moment that she might be the target of stalker. 'Haven't been on a bike for years.'

'Well, you know what they say.'

'You never forget, right? Like swimming.'

The Underground steps were ahead of them. Not allowing their pace to slacken, Tom ushered Laurie in front of him. Mingling with the other passengers and using their Oyster cards, they passed through the busy ticket barriers but still he couldn't help noticing that, after a brief respite, Laurie's nervousness had returned. She glanced back over her shoulder several times, and visibly flinched when a shaven-headed man in a white T-shirt pushed past her. 'No, it's all right, it's not him,' she said with an edgy smile. Then anxiously: 'You don't *really* think I'm being watched, do you?'

Tom gave what he hoped was an encouraging smile. 'Probably not. But to be realistic, there is a lot of stalking going on all the time. Maybe he's a weirdo and has a fixation on lady photographers, I don't know . . . What did you look like in the photos Gemma took?'

Laurie shrugged. 'Same as now I suppose.'

'So he has a fair likeness of you?'

With her back to the station wall, Laurie flicked through her mobile. 'Look, here's some Gemma sent me. They must be on her phone too, so he'll probably still have access, yes. I forgot they were still on here. I could have shown you before, though what it would have proved I don't know.'

A laughing, blonder version of Laurie smiled up at him from the phone. Yep, that would be her: attractive with serious eyebrows that made her arresting in a way that wasn't easily forgotten. The sensations of unease for her safety that had first started this morning in the café were making themselves even more uncomfortably apparent in a region he thought of as his heart. He didn't like the fact that this character was being so persistent. He had her phone number, he knew where she lived and that she was going to stay with her parents who lived in north Essex. If it was really Laurie he was after it was possible that he'd figure either Liverpool Street or Fenchurch Street stations were where she was headed.

Suddenly, he realised that somewhere along the line he had started to half-believe her garbled version of events. Unlikely though it seemed, Laurie had stumbled into something she had no idea how to deal with.

'Are you on Facebook or Twitter?' he asked abruptly.

Laurie shrugged. 'A bit.'

'What's that meant to mean?' he asked with a touch of impatience. 'Either you are, or you aren't.'

'Well,' said Laurie, her feistiness coming back at a stroke, 'no need to be so aggressive. It sounded like a good idea so I'm on there, but I can't say as I use it much.'

Right, so Snake-tattoo could gain entry to who knew how much more information about Laurie.

'Is that bad?' she asked.

'Well, not good, let's say.'

With a whoosh of hot air the train arrived. They found two seats, Tom put the holdall on the floor between them and Laurie rested her rucksack on her lap. He examined the pictures on her phone again. 'You ought to make yourself look different.'

She gave a dry laugh. 'Yeah, I thought plastic surgery might do it.'

Tom smiled. 'Easy for girls. You

already look a bit different.' He glanced from her to the picture on her phone and back again. 'Are you attached to your hair?'

Laurie blinked. 'Only in as much as it grows out of my head.'

'No, I mean the length of it? The easiest thing to do would be to get it cut really short; it's quite dark at the roots. That would make a huge difference. That and a pair of dark glasses. Your — your eyes are pretty . . . ' He stopped; he'd been going to say 'fantastic'. Hurriedly he changed it to 'memorable; although in a photo, of course, the colour's never clear.'

'You're really taking this seriously, aren't you?'

Tom felt his colour heighten. 'Look I'm just advising you, right? You don't have to do as I say. Whatever it is you're mixed up in, you need to be careful. If what you say is true and this character has already killed once and ordered a clean-up job, we could be talking gangs.' Tight-lipped, Tom sat back against the seat and watched as more passengers alighted from the train and others surged in.

Laurie turned a pair of frightened eyes towards him. 'Gangs?' she repeated faintly.

'And now,' continued Tom, 'Now, would be a good time to tell me if you *are* mixed up with anything illegal, be it drugs, firearms or whatever.'

Her eyes widened with surprise then darkened with fury. 'What? Of course I'm not. Why would I be? Oh, this is completely mad. First off you don't believe me, then we decide the guy has a penchant for stealing cameras, and now you seem to think I'm part of an Underground crime ring or something equally ridiculous. You're just unbelievable! No wonder no one wants to go to the police for help!'

Trying not to grin, Tom rolled with the punches. 'Keep your hair on. I had to ask. Now think a moment — what about your ex-boyfriend, the fashion photographer? A lot of his type end up hooked on drugs and they'll do all sorts in order to feed their habit. Maybe he stashed something in your camera case, and his contacts came to pick it up.'

'Absolutely not!' At first Laurie was vehement. Tom watched with interest, as she stopped and thought some more. Then she shook her head as though dismissing something she'd given fair consideration. 'No. Well, I really don't think so. Look, we met on the photography course. He's nice. Well, he *was* nice till he decided fashion photography was where the money was and started wearing poncey scarves and white trousers and things and calling everyone 'darling' and 'babe'. He could be a bit of an idiot. But drug dealing? No way!'

'You don't have a car, do you?'

'No. What's that got to do with anything, anyway?'

'I wonder if they know you don't have one.'

'Listen, my work as a photographer is hobby-based and spasmodic in the extreme. I work as a temp; currently I'm working at a call centre. I've got a mortgage on a flat in London — not a good post code, I know, but still expensive! I don't even have the money to get my roots done, as you so succinctly pointed out! Of course I don't have a car. Anyway, what difference would it make?'

'For a start, the difference between whether they take a short cut and go by road to your parents' place, and sit and wait for you to turn up, or watch out for you at the main stations and catch up with you there. That would be their easiest option. Same old thing; it all depends on how much they know about you.'

The lights on the train flickered briefly as it slowed, then suddenly started to pick up speed again. Laurie looked thoughtful. 'I thought that now everyone's on computer. You can pretty much find out whatever you want once you have a name . . . Although Kendal's not that common, I suppose.'

' 'Snake-tattoo', on the other hand . . . '
said Tom with a grin.

'Oh, ha ha! Wait a minute; we're going too fast now. Suppose it *was* the camera he wanted for some reason? Well, he's got it now. Why should he bother me any further?'

'If he's got what he wants, why has he phoned you since? Not to mention phoning your place of work.' He waited for her to digest that one. 'He wouldn't bother, would he? He'd just throw Gemma's phone away along with her rucksack, and that'd be an end to it.'

'Oh!' Then she smiled.

It took him a moment to recover from the stomach flip the smile caused. 'What's funny?'

' 'Place of work!' You sound so like a policeman.'

'Oh, ha ha!' echoed Tom.

They stopped at another station. Travellers got on and off: office workers with briefcases, tourists with maps, students in ripped jeans, even mothers with toddlers — goodness knew where they were going. Tom doubted whether any of them were anxious about being followed.

'The thing is,' went on Laurie when they were underway again, 'I'm not going to be able to help them anyway. I haven't got anything they could possibly want. So what do they plan to do with me when they find that out?'

'I do wish you hadn't asked that.'

'Oh!' said Laurie, looking anxious again. Perhaps he shouldn't have said that, but although he didn't want her scared to death she needed to be aware, if she wasn't already, that some criminals would stop at nothing.

'Depends what they're looking for, but if Gemma's been killed for no reason other than that she was *there* . . . Well . . . That's why I was serious when I suggested you make yourself look different. If I were you I wouldn't even go to your parents'. I'd go and stay with someone who has nothing to do with you, no connection with you at all. Haven't you got anyone like that?'

Laurie screwed up her nose in thought. 'I've got friends, of course I have, but right now they're slightly thin on the ground. My best friend's just moved in with her boyfriend.' Her nose wrinkled some more, and in some strange way Tom found himself more attracted to her than ever. 'They're all over each other; it's embarrassing. I really don't want to be a gooseberry. Another friend is a nurse and moved up north; another has landed a job as a fitness instructor on a cruise ship — it's just sailed from Southampton. Anyway, we're all on Facebook, so easily found I should think. Then there's Thursday's pub quiz team, but I don't know them well enough to flat-crash . . . No, it'll have to be my parents'.'

The journey was going fast. If he was going to his flat to pick up his bike, as was his original intention, it was only one more stop to where he should leave the train, and that would mean leaving Laurie alone. He looked at her side view and swallowed. Laurie was the sort of girl always worth a second glance. She would be noticed. If what she'd said was true, she was vulnerable; she had no idea how vulnerable. He shut his eyes and counted to ten.

'You could come with me.'

Her eyes widened in disbelief. Then with a dismissive gesture, she turned away. 'Yeah, right!'

'I mean it,' said Tom, aghast to find just how much he did mean it.

'I can't do that. I'd mess up your holiday.'

'It's already messed up. Besides, if you don't, I'll only worry about you.'

Laurie licked her lips. 'But you don't even know me.'

'I know. Makes it worse, doesn't it?'

★   ★   ★

Wordlessly, Laurie stared at him. It was only as he started to get to his feet that she realised how much she didn't want him to go.

'Anyway, I can't possibly come with

you,' she said, because she felt she must say something.

'And why's that?'

'I haven't got a bike.'

Tom looked at her seriously for a long moment out of his so-blue eyes. Then a wide grin spread across his face. 'No problem,' he said. 'I've got a spare. This is my stop. Are you coming or not?'

Laurie stayed where she was. She watched as with a shrug he swung his way to the doors of the train. She sat tight as the doors opened and he stepped onto the platform. If he hadn't turned as if to come back, she probably would have carried on sitting there, but he did — their eyes met, and suddenly, as though she had no will of her own, she found herself moving in her seat, struggling to pick up her holdall at the same time as manhandling her rucksack onto her shoulder, then hurtling to escape the compartment doors before they closed on her.

'Oh,' she said breathlessly when she'd

somehow stumbled onto the platform.

Saying nothing, Tom took her holdall from her. Their fingers touched just for a moment and she wondered whether she'd imagined the spark of electricity which made her disengage her fingers as though they'd been burned. For a moment he looked equally shocked, then turned quickly away from her and strode down the platform.

'Where are we going?' she asked the back of his yellow sports shirt when she'd managed to find her voice again.

'To my flat,' answered Tom. 'I'm going to look over my girlfriend's old bike. Then we're going to find a hairdresser.'

Laurie stopped dead in her tracks. 'Wait a minute. Your *girlfriend*'s bike?'

Tom glanced back over his shoulder. 'Well, technically, yes. My ex-girlfriend, actually, and I don't think she'll ever want it back. I've sort of hung on to it. Comes in handy from time to time. I'll check the brakes and give it a bit of an overhaul while you get your barnet sorted out.'

'My barnet? Oh, my hair.'

'Easier short for cycling anyway, and if you wear some wrap-around sun-glasses even your mother wouldn't recognise you. Snake-tattoo won't stand a chance.'

'I can't cycle through London. I'd be too scared.'

'Not asking you to. We'll take the bikes on the train.'

'Are you allowed to do that?'

'Trust me. I'm a policeman. Snake-tattoo won't be looking for two people on a cycling holiday together.'

It was all beginning to make some sort of crazy sense, but she couldn't help wishing Tom looked less as though in some way he'd found himself in the middle of a nightmare. For a moment there when their eyes had met, just before she'd got off the train, she'd thought . . . Well, she wasn't quite sure what she'd thought, only that he didn't want it to be 'goodbye' either. And then when their fingers had accidentally brushed, they'd both leapt as though they'd been stung. He'd turned away as though scared that if he didn't, he might do something rash and irresponsible. It was all very strange when they hardly knew, and certainly didn't like, each other . . . much.

'It'll give us breathing space,' he said. 'Give us some time to consider the options.'

But she did quite like the way he was saying 'we' and 'us'. Somehow it made her feel not so utterly alone.

Tom's flat turned out to be in a block, purpose-built as was Burleigh Mansions, but there the resemblance ended. This was a modern build, almost hostel-like with small rooms and low ceilings. He lived on the third floor and the apartment consisted of a tiny hall, a sitting room with a small kitchen area at one end, and a further two doors, which she took to be a bathroom and bedroom respectively, also leading off. It was all remarkably tidy, thought Laurie, looking round.

'Not much,' said Tom with a wry

smile. 'But I like to think of it as home.'

'It's nice,' said Laurie, taking in the one small bookshelf and the pile of cycling magazines on the coffee table. The décor was what might be described as bland: magnolia walls that were unadorned, apart from an acoustic guitar which hung on the shortest one; the floor throughout a laminated imitation wood sporting only one rug, which was porridge-coloured and sat in front of a brown leather cushionless sofa. There were no curtains at the windows, only plain blinds in another shade of magnolia.

Boring, boring, boring. No wonder the girlfriend was an ex, thought Laurie, who had conveniently forgotten for a moment that much the same thing could be said of her own home at present.

'We'd better go through your stuff first,' said Tom. 'It will have to go in your panniers over the back wheel. I hope you're prepared to travel light.'

Laurie looked at him for a long

moment. 'Has anyone ever told you you're bossy? No, don't answer that. I can travel light, but I'll bring my rucksack. It's quite small — it can go on my back.'

Tom glanced at it. 'D'you use it like a handbag?'

'Yes, you can get more in it than a small handbag and it's easy to carry. Besides it's quite on-trend as an alternative to a designer bag.'

'Thought you weren't into fashion.'

'Fashion's different. Fashion's for wimps. Trend and style, now that's the thing.' She cast a disparaging glance at his yellow sports shirt. 'You've either got it — or you haven't.'

Tom accepted the barb with a grin. 'All right, you can bring your rucksack and store a bit of light stuff in there, but you only need a few thin layers and your leggings will do. There's a jelly saddle on the bike, so that'll save your bum from getting sore.'

'Thanks a lot,' said Laurie sardonically before kneeling on the floor in order to sort out her things.

The sarcasm was lost on Tom. 'S'all right,' he answered. 'Now I'm going to the garage block to check your bike. I'll bring back your panniers; mine are already packed. We ought to get started as soon as possible.'

'What about my hair?'

'You can tuck it in your helmet until we find somewhere to have it cut, probably tomorrow.'

'Does that mean I have to keep my helmet on while I'm on the train?'

''Fraid so.'

Laurie sat back on her heels and watched as, whistling under his breath, Tom let himself out of the flat.

She looked around her again. What on earth was she doing? Why was she here, planning to go on a cycling holiday with a bloke she hardly knew — and a policeman at that?

Surely he was being a bit over the top, with all this cloak and dagger stuff? Surely she'd allowed herself to panic; to think, even for a moment, that she was being stalked, when there was no obvious reason for it? The only thing she'd had that was worth taking was the camera, and that had been taken already, hadn't it? If Tom really thought she was in danger, why didn't he march her to the police station and lock her in a cell? She'd be safe enough there, wouldn't she?

Then she chuckled inwardly, imagining that even if a police cell were available for the use of someone whose story was as flimsy as hers, the sort of fuss she would have made at the very thought of staying in a cell. Anyway, why should Tom disrupt a perfectly good holiday plan just for her, unless he believed her and was worried for her safety?

Laurie shrugged and went back to deciding which items of clothing were essential and which superfluous to requirements.

Throwing old tickets, shopping receipts, and interesting pamphlets she'd picked up from goodness knew where into her by-now half-empty holdall, she packed her phone; purse — thank goodness she'd just been paid and had money in the bank; small makeup bag containing one lipstick, one eye-pencil and a tube of moisturiser; her notebook and pen; and a packet of tissues into her rucksack. The small pile of clothes she'd put on one side to travel in the panniers was practical and uninspiring: one pair of jeans, one spare pair of leggings which could be washed and dried overnight, assorted long- and short-sleeved T-shirts, one sweater, and a few bits of underwear. Together with her bag of toiletries, that would do it. So long as the weather held up, she'd be fine.

'Well done,' said Tom when he came back with the panniers. 'We'll pack my spare cagoule. It'll be miles too big, but that doesn't matter; they haven't forecast rain anyway. Now, I've brought the map to show you.' He unfolded the cycle tour map. 'Most of these planned routes are one-day rides that circle back on themselves. I've sort of hinged the ones going north together. There's a choice of pubs to stay at. I've reserved a room already at the most popular places — just to be sure.'

Laurie tried not to blink. Now was not the time to start being picky about one room as opposed to two. She'd just have to cross those bridges as and when.

'We're going to have to cut out Rainham Marshes because of the time factor — we have a few hours to make up; but I'd still like to take in Abberton. I was there in March and the fields were full of skylarks. I've never seen so many.'

'Really?' she said with an attempt at enthusiasm.

'Yes, really. You know, one of those mornings — crisp and sunny, so still and quiet you could hear your own breath.'

Goodness, he'd nearly turned into a poet. Spellbound, Laurie watched Tom's face take on a dream-like quality as he continued to reminisce. 'Cold, but bright with a blue sky; the reservoir in the distance sparkling but completely tranquil . . . Then suddenly I could hear this birdsong and spotted flocks of skylarks climbing up into the sky singing all the way . . . ' He broke off as though embarrassed. 'It was awesome,' he finished.

'I'm sure,' said Laurie. 'No really,' she went on as he flushed. 'I didn't mean to be rude. I'm sure had I been there I'd have loved it. I think when you live in the city you appreciate the peace and quiet of the country much more. I don't often visit my parents, but when I do I always find time to walk on the fens. They're bleak but beautiful. I wish I knew more about birds really. I thought skylarks were a rarity?'

'They were a few years back. Getting better now. Did you know when they finish singing and climbing in the sky and drop down suddenly, they go straight to their nest in the grass? I came across one; it was filled with down and there were four speckled eggs inside arranged point to centre. Amazing!'

She met his eyes. So blue, and at that

moment quite serious. Suddenly it was difficult to tear her gaze away.

'Yes, well,' he said, clearing his throat and turning his attention back to the map. 'We might as well grab a coffee or something before we start out. We can take the bikes on the train as far as Chelmsford, have a spot of lunch and go on from there, maybe take in Fingringhoe, which is a nice little place, not too busy, but not Colchester — unless you particularly want to?'

'No, it's your holiday. We should do whatever you want,' said Laurie. 'Well, within reason,' she added as an afterthought, remembering the mention of a room, not rooms.

What was she doing blushing like a schoolgirl? Thank goodness Tom's attention was focused back on the map. Anyone would think she had the hots for him!

5

All in all, Tom was agreeably surprised.

At first he'd been appalled that in order to keep Laurie safe, he'd voiced the idea that she accompany him. But once said, he knew he couldn't possibly take the offer back, even though the only other time he'd taken a girl with him cycling it had been a complete disaster. Well, at least this time he knew what to expect: constant moans about the weather being too hot, too cold, too windy or too wet; unnecessary stops for proper toilets with hot water and mirrors; and, worst of all, the thing he hated above all else — a slow pace.

He hardly knew Laurie. She might be picky about her food, not have much stamina and keep up a constant tirade of 'how much further?'.

But so far none of that had happened. Contrary to his expectations,

Laurie had made no fuss about having her hair cut in a salon on the edge of Chelmsford, and even he had had a qualm about that because her shoulder-length hair, though wild, had been thick and, he had to admit, very lovely; the kind of hair that you'd like to wake up next to in the morning and just gently stroke. He smiled grimly at the thought and immediately forced the picture from his mind. But if Laurie had had any second thoughts when she'd seen her severed locks fall to the hairdresser's floor, she'd kept them to herself.

'Oh well,' she'd said with a shrug. 'I suppose it'll grow again.'

And despite himself, Tom had felt a stirring of admiration, because he knew that most girls with or without her kind of looks would throw a wobbly at the mere suggestion of sacrificing their long, luxurious tresses. But, drastic as it was, it had worked. With less of the amazing hair, Laurie's eyes seemed even more dominant, though there was no doubt she could now pass for one in a crowd, rather than stand out as a good-looker taking your breath away on first impact.

'Good job. Well done,' he'd said shortly.

Her only remark since then had been that her hair was a nuisance when she forgot about it being short and dragged her brush too far down her neck. 'Painful,' she said, pointing to the rough red patch on her collarbone. 'Mega-painful.'

The new cut did make her look quite different. As well as the colour change, back to her natural mid-brown, it had been styled asymmetrically, with a really short side but a longer piece at the front that dangled over one eye. It took Tom a while to get used to it, but he had to admit that because she had the bone structure and confidence to carry it off, it did look rather Frenchified chic. She didn't ask him what he thought, just grinned at him as she tucked the long piece of hair into her cycling helmet with an 'Easy-peasy!'

Prior to the haircut, the train journey to Chelmsford had been uneventful, with no sightings of Snake-tattoo or of anyone else taking the slightest interest in them. After the visit to the hairdresser, they'd taken the country roads out of Chelmsford towards Tiptree and Abberton as Tom had planned. At first he rode quite slowly, knowing that if he went flat out Laurie would soon be left behind. The terrain was easy going and although not built for speed, the bike she was using with its handlebar gears was reasonably easy to manipulate. He'd expected her to be a little nervous to begin with, and was agreeably surprised when she set off at a spanking rate he knew she wouldn't be able to keep up for long. Sure enough, she soon slowed down and from then on matched her speed to his. And although if he'd been alone he would have travelled much faster, he found he didn't really mind. In fact he quite liked thinking of her cycling along behind him and the odd passer-by maybe taking them as a pair.

From time to time, he glanced over his shoulder to reassure himself she was keeping up.

'You haven't shaken me off yet,' she said once cheerily, and on another occasion: 'You know I'm quite enjoying this — it's so peaceful.'

Even so, whenever they came to a cross road, Tom would stop and pretend to consult his map in order to give her time to catch her breath. Wordlessly he'd pass some water to her, covertly admiring the line of her throat as she drank.

After what he considered to be long enough for a novice, they stopped at a pub and Tom had a lager while Laurie greedily gulped down some orange. Carelessly, she removed her cycle helmet and ruefully ran her hand over her hair. 'Forgot it had gone for a minute,' she said.

'It looks great,' Tom found himself saying. Then, because he didn't want her to think he was paying her a compliment, which of course he was, but couldn't quite acknowledge that even to himself yet, he asked: 'Everything OK?'

'Why wouldn't it be?'

'Not finding it too much?'

Laurie gave him a stare. 'Of course not. I was born on a bike.'

'Really? That must have been uncomfortable for your mother.'

Laurie's half-laugh froze on her face. 'Oh dear, I haven't phoned her yet.'

'Why not? I thought you'd done that ages ago.'

'Well, I have been a bit busy,' she said belligerently. Then she sighed. 'I'll do it in a minute.'

Somehow, Tom got the idea she didn't really want to ring her mum. 'Is it a long time since you've been home?' he asked.

'Went when I first got back from Jo'burg. Not since though,' said Laurie in a subdued voice. 'We don't really have a lot in common. I mean she's my mum and all that, so of course . . . And my dad, well, he's . . . ' Her words trailed off.

Tom kept quiet. 'It's just . . . There's only me, you see, and I'm a bit of a disappointment. Oh, they weren't neglectful; far from it. They sent me everywhere; I did everything. Best schools, elocution, horse riding, ballet, clarinet lessons, singing lessons . . . ' She stopped for a moment. 'Oh dear, yes — the singing lessons! I hated them. My mother was full of hope I'd be the new Julie Andrews . . . They were struggling to find my talent, you see.' She gave a laugh. 'It must have been a bit of a blow to find I didn't have one.'

'What about your photography? Sounds like you're pretty passionate about that.'

Disconsolately, she shook her head. 'I enjoy it, yes, but it's not heart-and-soul stuff, not in the way they enjoy things.'

'What sort of things?'

Laurie stretched her tanned, shapely legs out in front of her and fiddled with her beer mat, then she glanced at him from under her lashes as though measuring whether or not to go on. She sighed and looked away. 'My parents have a marriage made in heaven. My mother's married to the local operatic society and my father's wedded to the golf course. They meet for drinks and the occasional dinner.' She glanced away, as though she'd said too much. 'Sorry, that's not entirely true. My dad's a successful businessman and Mum's very happy entertaining clients and arranging flowers when she's not appearing in *My Fair Lady* or something similar. I told you it was her dream that I became a successful musical star.' She grinned. 'I suppose I should be grateful she didn't call me Dolly, or Mame!'

About to take a swig from his beer glass, Tom paused and gave a chuckle.

'Yep, I don't really fit in very well. They're much more comfortable with me living in London than at home; my father even stumped up most of the deposit for my flat. And if that sounds ungrateful, I'm sorry, but that's how it is. They're always waiting for me to achieve something and I'm afraid to say

I never will. I somehow manage to hurtle from one mess to another, never settling on anything, never achieving anything.' She sighed. 'This is so typical of me — finding the wrong boyfriend, going with him to Jo'burg, falling out with him, struggling to survive out there and shacking up with a girl I hardly knew and didn't even like much. Then when I can come home, because the six-month let on my flat is at long last up, not being able to find a decent job ... Then getting mixed up in all this lot — whatever it is.' Her shoulders tensed and a frown line appeared above her nose. 'See what I mean? Not a daughter you'd want to boast about, am I?'

Suddenly, she looked vulnerable. Tom swallowed. 'I don't know about that,' he said. 'I'd say you've proved you have an independent streak and strong determination. No bad things, either of them. They're just giving you some room to do your own thing. Lots of people would love it if their parents backed off and stopped interfering.'

Laurie was silent for a moment, then looked up at him through thick makeup-free lashes.

'What about your family?'

'What about them?'

'I've told you about mine. It's your turn.'

Tom shrugged. 'Not a lot to tell. Large family. I'm one of five. Less pressure, I suppose. One of my sisters is a hairdresser; that's how come I know how much a hairstyle can alter a person's appearance. A woman's, at least. Not so much a man's. Unless he shaves it off, of course.' He smiled. 'Might find out pretty soon. Baldness runs in my family. My eldest brother's nearly there already.' He felt a moment's pride as he realised Laurie was laughing. She was looking relaxed again, and he was the person who'd caused this to happen.

'Right,' she said. 'I'll bear it in mind should I be looking to procreate.' Then she put her hand over her mouth. 'I can't believe I said that. I was joking. It just sort of came out . . . Sorry!'

'Nothing to be sorry for,' said Tom, amused to notice her blush and wondering if she'd ever considered the kind of banter that went on in a police station.

Laurie finished her drink in silence, then gave a small cough. 'About my parents. You're right, of course you are, about phoning them. I'm just putting off the evil moment, that's all. Tell you what, I'll ring them tonight when we get to wherever it is we're going to stay. I'll just make it casual. No talk of dead bodies or anything to make them freak. Yep, I'm on a cycling break with a friend and thought I'd call in for a couple of days, hey? Then I can take it from there. Maybe tell my dad later after I've gauged how things are shaping up. Yes, that's it.' She gave a sudden smile, and Tom's heart swelled a little in his chest. 'Thanks, Tom,' she said.

This time it was Tom whose face

reddened. He quickly looked down at the map in order to hide it.

*   *   *

At the end of the cycling day Laurie was amazed at how much she'd enjoyed herself. She now knew what people meant when they said they were bone-weary, but found she didn't care. They arrived at a small, clean pub where an extra room she was shown to was booked without fuss. After standing under a hot, sweet-smelling shower, she found that although every muscle ached in a way that wasn't entirely unpleasant, she had developed a ravenous appetite. Filtering from below was a mouth-watering aroma of garlic bread and possibly steak and onions, along with sounds of activity including the odd thump and laugh.

Suddenly she wanted to be down there in the friendly bar with Tom, sitting next to him, being thought of as at least his friend, if not his girlfriend

— and that wouldn't be altogether bad, would it? she asked herself. Her hair was damp but had fallen naturally into a half-decent shape. Even had there been a hair dryer available, she wouldn't have bothered with it. She dug around in one of her panniers and donned her jeans and a T-shirt that was low enough to reveal the warm glow she'd picked up from the sun whilst travelling. Then catching sight of herself in the mirror she hesitated, suddenly remembering her stupid comment about bearing him in mind for the purposes of procreation. She cringed. Very nearly flirting with him. What had she been thinking about?

It wouldn't do; it just wasn't on. Tom had only taken pity on her, for heaven's sake. He was doing her a favour. They'd become friends of a sort, and that was good, but that was all there was to it. Laurie made some resolutions. Only friendly banter from now on. No flirting, no holding his glance, no blushing every time he came close. He was a policeman doing his duty, maybe as a public-minded citizen first, but secondly as a policeman trying to protect the public — of which she was only one.

She rummaged in the pannier again and changed her T-shirt for one with a higher neckline. There, that was better. To give herself some confidence she hummed a short snatch of a popular song to herself before finding her way down the stairs to the bar. Yes, she could do this.

Tom was easy to spot. In the blue shirt that matched his eyes exactly, he was twenty years younger and twenty times more attractive than anyone else at the bar. Laurie's heart suddenly skipped a beat. *Calm down*, she told herself again. *He's a policeman, remember*.

'Hi!' His eyes creased at the corners in tune with his smile, which for the first time she realised was slightly crooked. But she decided she didn't mind crooked — not when it came to smiles anyway.

'Hi-ya,' she responded, slipping into the seat next to him.

'Like a drink?'

'Could kill a lager,' she said, eyeing the one that was sitting on the bar in front of him looking enticingly cool and refreshing.

He asked the barmaid for a repeat order and passed the menu over to Laurie. 'I recommend the steak and chips,' he said. 'Go on, you've earned it.'

'Sounds good to me.'

There was a convivial but laid-back atmosphere in the pub, which was small and countrified. Laurie eyed the dried hops festooned above the bar, the old sepia photos of various cricket teams arranged on the sloping walls, and the shabby upholstery so oddly at variance with the highly polished tables and chairs. There was a flagstone floor and a rag rug by the chimney breast on which a sleepy Labrador sprawled. Occasionally, between snores, he twitched his back leg.

It all felt surprisingly relaxed. She could hardly believe that only this morning she had felt so stressed and, yes, terrified. She stole a glance at Tom's profile. Suddenly she wanted to thank him but didn't know quite how. How on earth to tell him she felt she owed him her sanity and in fact even maybe her life? It was too much. He'd think she was being hysterical again, and he'd probably be right because she was so tired she couldn't think straight anyway.

'It's nice here,' she said eventually.

'Even nicer outside.' He picked up his drink from the bar together with the wooden spoon with their order number on the back. 'Come on, there's a duck pond outside and a floating duck island. Last time I came at about this time there were some baby ducklings. We might just catch them before they go to bed.'

She grinned. 'Shouldn't that be 'roost for the night'? I mean I'm no expert — you're the fountain of bird knowledge.'

'Don't be cheeky. Just pick up your

drink and follow me,' said Tom.

Just outside the door was a picnic table positioned to face the pond. They sat down next to each other with their backs against the warm bricks of the pub wall. The sun was just disappearing behind the trees on the opposite bank of the pond. The light streaks in the sky contrasted dramatically with the dark of the trees and the still, shadowed water. Silently a couple of ducks floated past, shattering the reflections of the willows into a thousand pieces.

Slowly Laurie let out her breath. It was so peaceful. After another appreciative moment, she turned her attention to her lager, first sighing in anticipation then drinking thirstily. 'Lovely.'

Tom raised his glass in order to do the same. 'Well, here's to the next couple of days or so.'

Laurie watched as he tilted his head back and swallowed the lager. There was a triangle of tanned skin showing a suspicion of chest hair between his shirt and the base of his throat. Firmly she tore her eyes away and set her glass down. 'I hope I haven't completely spoiled it for you.'

Tom contemplated his empty glass for a moment before answering. 'Hmm, nice. I'll get us another in a minute. What was that? Oh yes . . . No, you haven't spoiled anything. You're not too bad.' He stopped and his eyes did their crinkling trick again. 'For a girl, that is. I thought you'd be moaning all the time, but you haven't — so far.'

Taking in the tranquil view before her, Laurie shrugged. 'What's to moan about? I mean, you promised me ducklings . . . No ducklings, but other than that, I'd say it's pretty damn perfect. Isn't it?'

'Yes,' said Tom, gazing back at her. 'I'd say that right now it is . . . ' He broke off, then glanced back at the scene before them. 'Mustn't get too complacent though. Tomorrow it's up at the crack of dawn. We must press on.'

Laurie's heart sank a little. Of course, he just wanted to deliver her to her parents. Get shot of her. Not have to worry about her anymore. She was a fool to think he was enjoying this as much as she was.

'Two steak and chips. One rare, one medium rare!'

The two plates were placed before them and Laurie gave herself over to the application of mustard and salt and a small sprinkling of pepper on her tomato, before sinking her fork into her juicy-looking steak.

'Oh wow,' she said, closing her eyes in ecstasy.

★ ★ ★

Sitting so close, close enough for their thighs to nearly touch, Tom was struggling to keep a grip on reality. Just beneath the euphoria of being here next to this admittedly strange (but in a wonderful way) girl he had thought he was rescuing from danger in a completely professional manner, he was aware of the feeling of doom and disaster that was making itself felt in the area where his brain used to be. And when exactly had his brain turned to mush?

Was it when she'd tucked into her breakfast with such gusto? When she'd agreed to sacrifice her hair without a murmur? When she'd suddenly, at the last possible moment, hurtled out of the train and joined him on the railway platform? Or had it been even before that, perhaps the very first time he'd set eyes on her and registered her as a wild child totally out of his league, therefore denying all feelings of attraction between them?

The attraction was there now all right.

That the attraction would prove to be fatal, he had no doubt.

For nothing had changed, he reminded himself. She was still a wild child with a posh voice and no real sense of direction. Still out of his league. So what was he doing sitting here getting in over his head, loving every moment of it and wishing it would never end? He watched her face as she chewed another mouthful of steak, then swallowed and made a little sound of appreciation that he couldn't help smiling at.

'Mmm, lovely,' she said, glancing towards him. 'All that fresh air makes everything taste so much better.'

Her rather fierce eyebrows drew together for a moment and Tom suddenly realised that beneath them her tawny eyes were contemplating him suspiciously.

'Why are you looking at me like that?' she said.

'Like what?'

'Sort of dopey.'

Get out of that, Tom. 'No reason,' he said, wiping the dopey look from his face and pulling himself together fast.

'Well, you're putting me off my food. Just stop it.'

Tom grinned. 'Right. Just slightly amazed at the awesome speed you can devour a meal, that's all.'

'I'll have you know,' she started,

resting her knife but not her loaded fork on the side of her plate. 'I'll have you know . . . '

But cutting her off mid-sentence, her mobile shrilled, suddenly and loudly. Fear leapt into her eyes. 'D'you think it's him?'

'Well, if you don't answer it we'll never know.'

Abandoning the fork, Laurie fished in her rucksack and studied her mobile. 'It's Mum,' she said, her expression only fractionally less fearful. She put her phone to her ear. 'Hi, Mum . . . No, just eating dinner . . . Yep, fine. I was going to ring you . . . Yes, I was, honestly.'

For a couple of moments there was the sound of a female voice from the other end.

Laurie's magnificent eyebrows rose a notch. 'Oh, Dad's in Paris on business and you're up to your eyes in rehearsals for *Carousel* — and that's your favourite, isn't it? Now might not be a good time for me to visit, then.'

More feminine prattle, this time lasting much longer. Rolling her eyes, Laurie looked towards Tom apologetically, then her eyebrows pulled together again with concern. 'When's he back? Oh, a couple of days, right . . . Hang on, what friend? What did you say his name was? Mum, I don't have a photographer friend called Mark . . . Well, it's not my fault. I didn't give him your landline number. Why would I do that? I don't even know the bloke . . . Mum, I assure you I would know if I'd given out your number, and I'm sorry but I'm as much in the dark as you are. How long ago did he ring? Well, I hope you told him to get lost.' She bit her lip as she listened to her mother's reply. 'That's OK . . . That's good that you told him you weren't expecting me. No, that's absolutely fine. Yep, promise. Look, I'm in the middle of dinner now. I'll ring again in a couple of days, catch up again . . . Yeah, bye.'

Slowly she clicked off her phone, looked at her plate with no trace of her previous enthusiasm, and then raised a pair of frightened eyes towards Tom. 'He rang a couple of hours ago. How did he *know*? How did he find my parents' phone number? How did he know that was where I was headed? He's got there before us — he couldn't possibly have followed us; we were on bikes for goodness sake . . . I just don't understand.'

Tom didn't understand either. Didn't really want to, because this character was beginning to annoy him the way he was always one step ahead. Annoy him in one way but in another, well, perhaps he would have Laurie's company for a couple more days.

'He won't cause my mum any hassle, will he?'

'I doubt it. It's you he's looking for, not her. If he thinks she's lying I suppose he might watch the house for a bit, but it's you he's looking for, not your parents.' He watched as the logic of this sank in.

'D'you think his name really is Mark?

I mean, he has to have a name, doesn't he? Everyone does.'

Tom gave her a half-smile. 'Well, I have to agree, Mark sounds a lot more likely than Snake-tattoo.'

There was no answering smile in Laurie's eyes. 'This isn't funny, Tom. I'm scared.'

Yes, he could see that. 'So?' he asked.

'What d'you mean, 'so'?'

'Now what? Are you still going to your mum's?'

'No point. Dad's not there. My mum's in the middle of 'You'll Never Walk Alone'. Huh, fat chance. She would have the heebie-jeebies if I told her about this without my dad being there. Anyway, I told her I wasn't going.' Morosely, she picked at a cold chip. 'I don't know what I'm going to do.'

Trying to quell the feeling of warmth that was pervading his soul at the thought of possibly a few more days with her, Tom tore his eyes away from her lips, still glistening from the chips, and looked at her empty glass. 'Well, nothing we can do right now,' he said prosaically. 'I suggest another drink's in order, and that we should go inside if we want to avoid being bitten to death by gnats.'

Laurie allowed him to lead her back inside the pub, which by now was full of locals and tourists alike and where a steady stream of conversation was buzzing. Laurie stuck to his side like glue while he stood by the bar waiting to be served. He found he didn't mind. Quite liked it, in fact. He noticed a couple of fellows glance in their direction, then quickly back again at Laurie. Oh yes, she was a looker all right. He must have been nuts to think that a haircut would stop her attracting attention.

They found a quiet corner table that had only just been vacated and sat down facing each other with their drinks between them.

'What will we do?' asked Laurie.

Oh how Tom loved that 'we'. 'Carry

on cycling,' said Tom. 'That would make a good name for a film, don't you think?'

Laurie pulled a face. 'Funny. Not very. It's all right for you.'

'How d'you make that out?'

'One, you're a bloke. Two, you're a policeman, although not a very good one as far as I can make out. Three, it's not you he's after. Four, you're on holiday and can go back to your neat, boring little life at any time you want.' She looked away, blinking.

'Laurie,' said Tom, and he had to physically grip one fist with the other in order to stop from reaching across the table for her hand. 'I'm sorry. I didn't mean to belittle the situation. I just don't see the point in panicking. He obviously has no real idea of where we are right now. You're right, he didn't follow us; he took a gamble that you'd run to your mother's.' He sighed. 'It's all too easy. After Googling you and finding out what part of the country you come from, he probably looked

149

Kendal up on the electoral roll and then phoned round. There's so many ways of finding people who have nothing to hide. Honestly, the general public have no idea.'

'Thanks a lot. I feel better already,' said Laurie darkly.

'Oh come on, you've enjoyed today, haven't you? I've got the map here. Let's look at our route for tomorrow.' He took the map, already neatly folded to the right section, from the pocket of his well-worn jeans, and placed it on the table between them.

'I'm sorry too,' said Laurie after a long moment in which she seemed to be struggling to find the right words. 'What I said about your being boring and a policeman. You're not boring.'

'I am a policeman, though, right?'

She looked at him appraisingly. 'Yeah. Funny, that. Did you *always* want to be a policeman?'

'Pretty much.'

'Why?'

Tom looked at her searchingly in case

she was laughing at him and was surprised to find that he could only discern interest in their depths. 'That's tricky,' he said. 'Wanted to help ordinary people, I suppose.'

'Right wrongs?'

'Bang wrong-uns up, give ordinary law-abiding citizens a chance.'

'And does it work like that?'

'Most of the time.'

'Isn't it dangerous?'

Tom laughed. 'Sometimes, but so is crossing the road.'

'Not if you use the green man.'

'No answer to that.'

'I envy you.'

Tom looked at her in astonishment.

'No, I do. You know what you want. Me? I'm rudderless. Just drifting . . . I mean, it's not fair.' For a horrible moment Tom thought he'd seen tears glisten in the tawny eyes, but she waved her hand in front of her face. 'What I mean is, you didn't ask for any of this and here I am being a pain in the neck.' She looked away, but when she looked back Tom was relieved to see she was smiling. 'Yeah, you're right. Let's enjoy the holiday why don't we? There's no earthly reason why Snake-tattoo should know where we are, is there? He's not clairvoyant.'

It was with the utmost determination that Tom kept his answering confident smile on his lips. The last thing he wanted to do was admit to Laurie that he'd suddenly realised exactly what he would have done had he been in Snake-tattoo's shoes and wanted to find out where Laurie was heading.

And if he was right, it would only be a matter of time before he caught them up.

6

In agonisingly slow motion she was walking into her flat. Her legs ached and her feet felt as though they were encased in concrete boots. But it wasn't much further; he'd said so. Hadn't he? A shiver started at the base of her spine, finishing at the nape of her neck where her hair lay sticky with sweat. Aware suddenly that she wasn't alone, she paused on tiptoe outside her bedroom door. Slowly she turned. A scream started in her throat but stuck there with the tenacity of a fish bone, refusing to travel further.

Gemma!

It couldn't be — yet it was!

Her head tipped at a curiously strange angle, *Gemma* was standing behind her, smiling that annoying smile of hers in the half-light.

But this was mad. Gemma was dead, wasn't she?

In her sleep Laurie whimpered and tried to move, but her limbs were too heavy to lift. Beneath her lids, her terrified eyes swept round her surroundings. It was definitely her flat. She recognised the half-dead pot plant on the cabinet. Half-dead. That was what it was — Gemma was only half-dead, while Laurie had thought for a while she'd been murdered. She almost cried with relief and stirred a little.

Murdered, murdered, murdered!

She woke with a violent jerk. Sweating and thirsty, she had to force herself to lie still for a moment. Slowly her breathing quietened and her heart rate went back to its normal pace.

She gave a shuddering sigh. Thank God it had only been a dream. Then on the heels of this realisation came the knowledge that real life was no less disturbing. On one elbow now, she groped for her side light and switched it on. When her heart had quietened some more she reached for the glass of water on her side table and sipped at it. With waking came the reality in all its awfulness. Gemma had been murdered. No matter what anyone tried to tell her, she'd seen the body — there was no room for doubt there, even though it seemed she was the only one who knew it for a fact.

All day she'd been suppressing the only-too-vivid pictures of a still and lifeless Gemma that lingered in her brain. Now in the depth of the night they'd come back to haunt her, big-time. In an effort to dispel the image of Gemma's ghostly face with her blue lips twisted into a ghastly smile, Laurie rubbed at her eyes. She was too tired for this, too raw, too lonely. Her head felt as though it contained a spinning top and, as though in stressful competition, her stomach had joined in the dizzying dance.

Determinedly, Laurie punched the pillow, turned out the light and focused on relaxing her body from the toes up. Concentrate on the positives, she told herself. She had Tom on her side after all, and even if he was still reserving judgement on the truth of what she'd told him, there was something very comforting and solid about Tom. Not to mention attractive and sexy, added another part of her psyche. She attempted a smile in the dark. Now was not the time to be thinking about that, but it was a whole lot better than the alternative nightmare she'd just woken from.

A yawn caught up with her. Despite everything she was so, so tired. And still thinking about Tom — the way his mouth lifted a little more on one side than the other when he smiled; the way his eyes twinkled when he found something amusing but didn't want to comment; the way, when his hand touched hers or their arms brushed, she really wanted nothing more than to move in closer and rest in the comforting circle of his arms.

It was all too ridiculous to contemplate.

Still smiling as she recalled her feeling of security at just standing next to him downstairs in the bar, she drifted off into a less troubled sleep.

★   ★   ★

But by the next morning Laurie's feeling of well-being had faded to the point of being nonexistent. For a start, she ached all over. Secondly, on first waking she'd forgotten about her hair, or the lack of it, so did a double-take when she glimpsed it in the mirror and realised afresh just how different she looked. Tom had changed her from wild child to primary-school teacher. She wasn't sure she liked the idea.

Then she noticed the swollen grey sky, and the thought of getting on a bike again developed a distinctly non-appeal factor. And that was Tom's fault too.

She'd allowed herself to think for a short while yesterday — no, that was wrong; for almost all day, actually

— that she and Tom had become friends. That he was, if not exactly her knight in shining armour, then at least her comrade in arms. But suddenly in the cold light of a grey dawn she reminded herself that, as a matter of fact, she hardly knew him. That whereas he seemed to know pretty well everything about her, she knew next to nothing about him.

Oh yes, she couldn't fail to notice that it was quite nice to watch his firm buttocks and strong legs and shoulders doing their stuff as he cycled along in front of her, but she still knew little about what was going on in his head. And towards the end of last evening she had suddenly had the sense that he was keeping something from her, although she could hardly begin to imagine what that something could be. What, after all, could he possibly know that she didn't?

No, she was overreacting as usual. Poor Tom; he'd realised anew that he was lumbered with her for a few days more and was trying to put a brave face on it. Because now instead of the initially planned route of Chelmsford, Abberton, Wivenhoe, Lavenham, then on to Bury St Edmunds, where there would be a parting of the ways, he'd chosen to change it. Later in the evening when she finally got to study the map and realised the distances involved, Laurie had argued that as they were already past Wivenhoe and headed in the right direction, they should stick to the original plan, go on to her parents', and she'd make a clean breast of it to her mother.

Tom had disagreed. 'I'll just adjust the route; we'll turn off here,' he said, pointing his finger on the map. 'You'll just have to stick with me a bit longer. No problem.'

Laurie looked where he was pointing. 'But that's the wrong way,' she said. 'We need to go left not right.'

'You mean west not east.'

'Whatever. All right, why do we have to go east then?'

'Because that's what I intended to do

after I'd dropped you off at Bury St Edmunds. My plan was to head cross-country — that's 'right' to you — and call in at Aldeburgh; but we'll do that first, and give Snake-tattoo the slip just in case he's doing a stake-out for you at your parents' place. He'll give up after a day or so. Bound to.' He turned his eyes towards her. 'I thought we'd already agreed all this?'

Laurie looked at where his finger was resting on a point that appeared to be miles away on the east coast. 'That was after speaking to Mum. I was panicking. I'm not now, though; I've calmed down. I'm thinking more rationally now. When I get to my parents' everything will be fine. If Snake-tattoo turns up, I'll . . . I'll phone the police.'

Tom said nothing, but his face said: country police? Do me a favour!

'Anyway,' she went on, her eyes back on the map, 'it's such a long way out of our way. Why to Aldeburgh? Something special there?'

'Just some people I know. It'll fill in

160

the time until your father gets back. He can decide what's best for you.'

The story of her life. 'Oh!' said Laurie, because nothing else that was polite sprang to mind.

Thinking back over the conversation now, she knew she'd sounded subdued because really there was no argument. Tom was in charge; he was the one to call the tune. But now she wasn't so sure. It seemed ridiculous to her to be travelling miles in the wrong direction, especially when her shoulders ached and the clouds above looked as though they were just waiting for her to step out of the door and lower the aching bones in her bottom onto her bike saddle before they dumped their cold, wet contents all over her.

Nevertheless, she found herself packing her panniers and her rucksack and, trying to look as though she really didn't mind the thought of an uncomfortable day in the saddle travelling the wrong way, she went down the stairs to join Tom for breakfast.

He'd already started on his. 'Morning,' he said briefly, in the act of spearing a sausage. 'Thought you weren't going to make it.'

'Wrong then,' said Laurie, hardly smiling because she'd forgotten for a moment how much she liked him and really didn't want him to know.

Tom gave a grin as an answer. 'I ordered you a full breakfast. It's coming up any minute.'

'Thank you.' Laurie helped herself to tea and a piece of toast just as her breakfast plate arrived.

'I've checked the weather. Hopefully those clouds will blow away.'

Laurie didn't comment. Those clouds still looked pretty threatening to her. But the bacon was good, the toast was hot and nice and thick, and she was hungry.

She looked up and caught Tom watching her with an amused expression. 'I see you're on the same diet as yesterday.'

'Ha Ha. Sometimes you can be quite

funny when you stop being serious Mr Plod.'

Tom laughed. 'You're very rude, Posh Girl! Mr Plod! How insulting! I'm wounded.'

'Sorry. Didn't mean to upset you,' said Laurie with her mouth full.

Tom gave an easy grin. 'Just showing you my sensitive side in case you thought I didn't have one.'

Laurie gave him a look and continued with her breakfast.

Once they'd finished Tom didn't take much time to get to his feet. 'Come on, we need to make a move.'

Laurie grimaced as she attempted to rise from the table. She groaned. 'I don't think I can. I ache all over.'

'I'm good at massage,' said Tom, quick as a flash.

'You're so thoughtful, but . . . no.'

'Let's get cracking, then. I've checked the bikes.'

'Right.' Trying to dispel images of exactly how a massage given by Tom might progress, a pink-faced Laurie obediently followed him out of the dining room.

★　★　★

Despite the threatening skies, the rain held off until mid-day. Laurie supposed she should be grateful for that at least, but she didn't feel grateful; she felt tired and fed up. Moodily she focused ahead, concentrating on keeping up with Tom who, it suddenly seemed, was treating this as a practice session for the Tour de France. Well, she wasn't going to let him think she was flagging. No way. Resolutely she forced her aching calves to pump even faster.

The rain continued to hold off and they had a comfort break at about noon. At least, Tom referred to it as a comfort break, although as far as Laurie was concerned there was nothing remotely comfortable about it. The pub had peeling paint and the toilets weren't exactly salubrious. Laurie used a couple of wet wipes on her hands before accepting a bag of crisps and a coffee, which thankfully came in a cardboard cup.

'Cheer up,' said an irritatingly optimistic Tom. 'The terrain around here's lovely and flat, really easy going, don't you find?'

'Yeah, nothing to it,' replied Laurie through gritted teeth. 'Now where's that sun you promised me?'

Tom didn't answer, just looked shifty.

Laurie burst out laughing. 'You really must think I'm stupid. Please credit me with a brain cell or two. It's going to get heavy, right? Stormy, in fact?' She looked at the sky. 'In less than half an hour I'd say. That's why you've been doing a Chris Hoy challenge, right?'

'We've got cagoules.'

'Just as well. How much further till we can stop at a decent pub?'

A cagey expression came over his face. 'Not sure.'

'Not sure?'

'Well, it was all a bit last-minute . . . I think I can remember one near Sutton

Hoo which isn't too far out of our way. We could visit Sutton Hoo while we're at it. It's an Anglo Saxon Royal burial site — sixth century I think. I'd planned to go anyway, but by myself, after I'd dropped you off.'

Laurie sighed. 'Can't wait,' she said. 'Will it be dry? Will there be tea?'

Tom grinned. 'That's better. Thought for a minute you were going to go soft on me. There's a museum there — it's fascinating.'

Laurie thought she'd reserve judgement on that one. Yesterday, their brief visit to Abberton had been lovely, with the blue skies and the birds, the peace and quiet and the carrot cake. Today though, the thought of poking about in an old burial site under heavy skies did not sound quite so inviting. But this was Tom's holiday, and it was what he wanted to do. She'd already messed it up for him, so she kept her thoughts to herself.

'OK.' She reached for her helmet. 'I'm ready when you are.' She gave a wide grin and moved towards the bikes. The sooner they got on the road the sooner they'd be there.

★ ★ ★

Tom knew she was annoyed.

He frowned. Maybe 'annoyed' was the wrong word. Restless, agitated? Agitated — yes that was it — and in trying to cover it up she was blaming anything rather than admit that she was scared again. The carefree, almost magical mood that had materialised yesterday had disappeared. Magical! What was he going on about? A bit of sun, a couple of lagers and a seat by a river — hardly magical! Anyway, it had vanished. Reality, like the rain, had caught up with them.

While she'd been using the ladies', Tom had rung the station to see if any bodies had turned up answering to the description of an Aussie called Gemma. Not so far, he'd been told by Judith Morgan. 'I shouldn't think there will be either. That girl was a nutcase.'

Tom didn't answer, just gripped his phone harder.

'Where are you, exactly?' she'd asked.

'At a rotten pub at the moment, but the next stop near Woodbridge should be better.'

'Well, enjoy yourself in your own solitary way. See you when you get back.'

'Sure,' said Tom. 'Thanks.'

The sky got no less threatening. Laurie made a valiant effort to speed up. Really, for someone who hadn't been on a bike in a long time she was doing pretty well, he acknowledged to himself. Even he was feeling the odd twinge in his back, and he was in pretty good condition, so she must be hurting all over.

But regardless of this, Laurie's pace didn't slacken and they reached Sutton Hoo in time to walk around the site and visit the museum. Once she was off her bike for a while Laurie seemed to buck up and, even if it was mainly the gold and jewellery that claimed her attention, she took an interest in the artefacts that Tom pointed out.

He enjoyed it too. He'd looked forward to exploring on his own but found that having Laurie there with him was rather pleasant. It helped that she never once complained of being bored. Yes, for a woman she was turning out to be quite good company, even if he did fancy her rotten; because, in spite of fighting it, he admitted the extent of his attraction to her now. Well, he'd have to be made of stone not to respond to some degree, he argued to himself. After all, she was easy on the eye, had a good sense of humour, didn't moan and whinge, and seemed to quite enjoy physical exercise — all very important things in Tom's book. Added to which, there was no doubt she had a certain other quality. He hated to call it the X-factor, but at the moment that was the only name he dared to put to it.

And now here she was standing next to her bike which, to be fair, was not built for speed in the way that Tom's was. She was looking if not exactly eager, then resigned, to mounting it again.

'How many more hundreds of miles is it?' she asked just as a few spots of rain started.

Tom didn't answer; just helped her on with her cagoule before shrugging into his own bright yellow one.

She raised an eyebrow. 'Canary yellow your favourite colour, then?'

'Only sensible on the road,' he replied gruffly. 'You've got to be bright to stay out of trouble.'

'Yeah.' Laurie put her hand to her eyes surveying the almost empty road. 'I can see that.'

'Can't be too careful.'

★ ★ ★

And he was right, admitted Laurie half an hour later when the few spots of rain had changed to a heavy downpour which felt as though it was driving horizontally straight into her face. It also made her aware how slippery the road was and how comparatively narrow her tyres were.

Resolutely she pressed on.

Her knees were wet and sore where they chafed against the too-big cagoule. There was water in her eyes and dripping off her nose, her hands felt frozen to the bike handlebars, and the small incline ahead took on the accessibility of Mount Everest.

One two, one two. *It's all his fault. I could be in Bury St Edmunds now with only a hot cup of tea and my mother's practice scales to contend with. Think I could manage that! What am I doing here?* Her thoughts rambled on. *Snake-tattoo must be a figment of my imagination. Even if he's not, he can't be interested in me. This is all just a terrible mistake; a nightmare. I'll wake up in a minute.*

Oh dear, the gap between them was widening. Why did he have to go so fast? All right for him on his state-of-the-art, feather-light speed machine with a hundred or so gears!

I hate Tom. Pedal down. *I hate Tom.* Pedal up. *I hate Tom!*

There was a sudden roaring in her ears. A hiss of water coming from behind, a grinding gear change, and a large, dark shape lumbered past.

For a fraction of a second, Laurie took her eyes off the road.

It was just enough to cause her front wheel to wobble. Her head veered forward, her bottom left its seat, her handlebars went sideway,s and she crashed over onto the grass verge.

A couple of seconds after landing she realised that lying here feeling sorry for herself wasn't the best way to deal with her bike, which was still in the road. Shakily she attempted to get to her feet.

'Take it steady,' said a calm voice behind her. 'I'll get your bike.'

Gratefully, Laurie sank back in a sitting position and put her head in her hands. She was feeling a bit sick.

'Bike's all right. What about you?' asked Tom.

'Oh don't worry about me, Tom. Glad you've got your priorities right. My arm's probably broken, but that's only a little thing, right?'

Tom grinned. 'That's the spirit. Well done. At least you had the presence of mind to fall the right way . . . Maniac driver! He didn't give you enough room and his lorry's far too big to be on this road.' He turned his attention back to Laurie. 'Your leg's bleeding. Let me see it. I bet your hands are stinging too.'

'I'm all right, actually,' said Laurie, quite surprised to find that now the nausea had passed it was true.

'Nevertheless . . . ' Tom knelt down and took her calf in his hands. 'Hmm, yes, only a graze. We'll clean it up at the pub. How about your hip? You must have given it a wallop.'

'Well, a bit, but it feels OK.' She looked down at her grazed knuckles and red and stinging palms. Now was not the time for bravery. 'My hands do hurt though. I'm not sure I can ride any further.'

'Nonsense,' said Tom. 'You're ready for another couple of miles, aren't you? Just remember at the end of it there'll be a nice hot shower and a tot of brandy.'

'Don't like brandy.'

'No pleasing you, is there? You'll be fine. Come on, I'll help you up.'

Instead of holding her by her poor, painful hands, he lifted her by her elbows. Suddenly she was standing close, too close, but not quite close enough. Entirely of its own volition, her heart started doing a strange dance.

Tom seemed to have stopped breathing. He was staring at her, his eyes taking on a traumatized expression. Perhaps they were both having a heart attack.

It only lasted a moment or so because just as Tom lowered his head towards her, Laurie felt her legs give way. He caught her seconds before she hit the ground again.

'S-sorry,' she said.

'It's shock. My fault; I should have given you longer.'

Laurie put her head in her hands

again. She felt like having a seriously good cry. A few tears would never be noticed in this weather, but the sort of howling she had in mind right now would leave her with red, swollen eyes and a runny nose.

Not a good look Laurie. Pull yourself together.

'I'm fine. I'm fine.' She extracted herself from his arms and sat back down on the so safe grass verge. It was surprising how attached you could become to a patch of wet grass.

They sat on the side of the road and watched a few cars go by.

'Idiot driver. I wish I'd taken his number,' said Tom.

'I probably wobbled a bit.'

Tom patted her hand. 'You probably did, but drivers should always be aware of cyclists' wobbles. That's better,' he went on as Laurie had a shot at a small smile.

'Yep. I'm OK now.'

'Are you sure? We can sit here a bit longer.'

'Are you kidding? We'll both die of pneumonia. Anyway, I'm hungry.'

And strangely, although she'd dreaded getting back on the bike, she found she was quite steady and oddly elated by the whole experience. Or perhaps it wasn't the experience of the tumble itself, but the euphoria of surviving both the accident and its aftermath when Tom . . . Well, who knew what had been on his mind for those dangerous few seconds where they'd stared at each other and the world had stopped?

The two miles passed more quickly than Laurie would have believed possible. Perhaps that was what shock did to you. Apart from making you vulnerable, it made your body clock slightly demented.

Tom indicated that he was turning right and they pulled into the courtyard of a pretty country pub, which would look attractive and welcoming at any time but right now, at the end of a physically and mentally tiring day, to Laurie looked like utopia.

'Oh, wow!' she said. 'Hot water, here I come.'

Tom helped her take her rucksack from her back. 'Oh dear,' he said, noticing a thread hanging loose from the bottom seam. 'You must've bashed it when you fell.'

Laurie gave it a cursory glance. 'No, it's been like that for ages. Cheap and cheerful, what can you expect? I think it happened when it went through the scanner at the airport.'

Tom bent to loosen the panniers over her back wheel. 'Just as long as you don't lose anything through it.'

'You sound like my mother.'

'Just as long as I don't look like her. Oh sorry, no offence meant. I don't know why I said that — never even seen her.' For the first time since she'd met him, Tom looked embarrassed.

'Just go and book us in.' Laurie heaved her rucksack onto her shoulder and picked up one of her panniers. Tom took the rest of the stuff and they walked into the pub looking like two drowned rats.

There was a small unoccupied nook just inside the door and to the left. Laurie made a bee-line for it and collapsed into one of the carver chairs. She heard Tom go through to reception, which was in the bar, and start explaining they'd had an accident. Then she zoned out until she heard the word 'tea'. She unzipped her cagoule, opened her rucksack, found a pack of tissues and wiped the rain and dirt from her face until she felt a little more presentable. Her hair under the hard hat was still fairly dry, so she fluffed it up with her fingers.

Tom came towards her, grinning. 'Two mugs of tea coming up right now; the landlady had just made a pot. And someone's getting our room ready.'

'Great,' said Laurie. Then her smile froze. 'What d'you mean *our* room?'

'Well, the good news is tea's coming. The bad news is there's only one double room left, I'm afraid.'

Laurie gave him a long look. 'Right, well, that'll suit me. Don't know what you're going to do though.'

'For goodness sake. What d'you think I'm going to do? Ravish you, like some Victorian scoundrel?'

'No, because you won't be there.'

They glared at each other until the clink of china announced the arrival of tea.

'Oh, lovely,' said Laurie.

'Yes, Lulu was just ready for that, weren't you Lulu?'

It took a moment for Laurie to realise she was being referred to as 'Lulu'. Deciding to put this revelation on hold for a moment, she thanked the bustling landlady and warmed her hands on her mug. Could this day get any more bizarre?

'Lulu?' she hissed as soon as the nook was empty again. '*Lulu?*'

'Well, I'd started the L already and I had to think of something.'

'What's wrong with the name Laurie? Apart from the fact that you associate it with a motor vehicle, of course.'

Tom looked shifty for a moment. 'I

thought we'd go under assumed names.'

Laurie rolled her eyes. 'Might one enquire why?'

'Just being thorough.'

'Paranoid, you mean. Just a minute.' Laurie narrowed her eyes. 'D'you know something I don't?'

Tom's eyes slid away from hers. 'Not really. It's all supposition.'

'D'you think you could share this 'supposition' with me?'

Tom picked up his steaming mug and sighed. 'I just put myself in Snake-tattoo's shoes and wondered what I'd have done if I was looking for you. He knows what you look like from a photo, which means you could be much taller or shorter, with a bigger build, etcetera. But he still has a facial resemblance. He knows the agency you work for, your London address and probably your parents' address too. We know most of that information came from Gemma's phone. He's trying to find *you*. He thinks you've got something he wants, right?'

Laurie nodded.

'You don't appear to have been at your London address all night. Who else can he ask about your movements? Ask yourself, who else would know? He revisits your flat. Nothing. What now? He looks around. Ah, there's a small café across the road; how very convenient. In he goes, orders tea. The Polish lady who runs the place is very chatty, very pleasant. He soon makes a friend of her. Oh, he tells her, he's just missed his friend Laurie who lives in the flats across the street. He knew she was going on holiday but somehow must have got the day wrong. Any ideas?'

Laurie's eyes widened. It was only too likely. 'Oh no,' she groaned. 'I told Pilar everything. Told her I was going to my mum's, where they live — everything . . . I always talk to her; she's so friendly so nice. But I didn't tell her about going with you, did I?'

'You didn't have to. She saw us together, she knows I'm a policeman, she knew I was going on a cycling holiday. You're not the only customer she talks to! She might even have mentioned that we left together.'

'So?'

'So we have to be even more careful, that's all. He's still got to take a sweep of the area, but hopefully he'll think we're taking the straightforward route.'

'So *that's* why we're going the wrong way?'

'It seemed like sense. Especially when I knew your father was away.'

'I wish you wouldn't keep doing that.'

'What?'

'Indicating that I can't look after myself.'

He didn't answer that. Didn't need to, realised Laurie. It was obvious he thought she was a hopeless case. She blinked and turned her head away.

'It's not that bad,' said Tom. 'You have the advantage, remember. You've seen him in the flesh. He's only seen your photo. Big difference . . . He'll probably phone round the pubs searching out a pair of cyclists. That's what I'd do.'

'You're making me nervous.'

Tom grinned. 'Me too. I'm making me nervous. That's why — 'Lulu'.'

'Yeah but — Lulu!' Laurie changed her attempt at a smile to a face of disgust. 'What's your name? Trevor?'

'No, Toby. I had to keep the T; it's on my card.'

'Toby,' she tried the name out. 'Toby. It's all right, actually — a bit like a dog's name, but not as bad as Lulu!'

'There aren't many boys' names beginning with T,' Tom said defensively.

'Tarquin?'

'Oh yes. I look like a Tarquin, don't I?'

Laurie put down her mug. A sudden shiver overtook her and her smile faded. She glanced round warily and lowered her voice. 'I don't like this. I don't like this one bit. I'm the only one who knows, I mean *really* knows Gemma is dead, right?'

Tom shot her a particularly searching look. 'Seems so. I called the station this morning. Gemma hasn't turned up

— dead or otherwise.'

'What does that prove?' retaliated Laurie, who had noticed the look. 'That I'm lying? You still don't trust me, do you?'

'Be reasonable. Would I still be here now if I didn't? Look, we need to go over everything again with a fine-toothed comb. There must be something of Gemma's you have that he still wants.'

Slowly Laurie shook her head. 'D'you think I haven't racked my brains over and over? All I've got of Gemma's is some lousy knitting.'

'Wait a minute. What did you say?'

'Knitting. She talked me into it. Gave it to me to do on the plane.'

Tom narrowed his eyes. 'I saw it at your flat . . . Ignored it as insignificant.'

Laurie clapped her hand to her head. 'Go on; tell me you think she's smuggling drugs in the middle of a ball of wool!'

'Well, I suppose it's possible.'

'Not . . . Actually, I can knit. I did knit. I finished the ball of wool on the flight. No drugs, not even a cod liver oil tablet. So what do you think of that, Sherlock?'

'Well, of course,' Tom blustered, 'you're right. Of course she couldn't possibly get enough drugs in there for it to be worth Snake-tattoo going to these lengths to recover. I'm just keeping an open mind, that's all.'

Laurie laughed weakly. 'A woolly, mind if you ask me. Oh come on. Knitting? Woolly? Get it?'

'Very funny. What are you knitting?'

'A cushion cover,' she answered with pride.

'Good Lord.'

'Knitted cushions are very on-trend and this one's easy. You start with one stitch and increase one at each end, but you slip one first. It's all plain knitting, no purl involved. Then, when you reach the middle you've got loads of stitches and you do the same thing backwards, decreasing instead of in-creasing — but you still slip the end stitch of course.'

'Of course.'

'It's going to look quite good, actually.'

'I'm sure,' said Tom, looking as though he was unable to believe he was really discussing knitting.

'There's another stitch called basket stitch,' went on Laurie relentlessly. 'You do ten stitches plain, ten purl for ten rows, then ten purl and ten plain. It comes out like a basket. It's very effective.'

'Really?' said Tom faintly.

Laurie gave him a wicked grin. 'You've no idea, *Toby*, how refreshing it is to speak to a bloke so in touch with his feminine side. Usually if a conversation's not about football or computer games they just don't want to know. I could teach you, if you like . . . Knitting, I mean.'

The landlady stuck her head round the nook. 'Your room's ready.'

'Lovely,' said Laurie and a dazed-looking Tom together.

As they gathered their things together,

Laurie sneaked a sideways look at Tom. 'Honestly, knitting's very good for the brain. Miss Marple used to do it all the time.'

7

Obviously, Laurie was talking nonsense — about knitting, of all things — to cover her discomfort; but Tom was aware that the grim smile he'd plastered to his features was only thinly disguising his embarrassment. Embarrassment was a state that in the past he'd seldom experienced, but then Laura was a girl like he'd never known before, and he had no idea how to handle this weird situation.

There was only one bed.

The landlady pointed out the tray of tea things, the small en-suite, the lovely view of the surrounding countryside, and the new flat-screened television. Then she gave them the time they could start ordering food downstairs that evening and told them when breakfast started next morning.

There was a gap called night-time

between the two.

'Water should be lovely and hot,' she said. 'See you later.'

When she'd gone, there was still only one bed.

'Not even a bath or a chair. It'll have to be the floor,' said Laurie as though she could mind-read. 'Either that or we share, and you leave your newly sharpened sword between us.'

He looked at her to see if she was joking. From her tone it was impossible to tell.

She continued to look at him without the vestige of a smile. 'That's what Lancelot did when he had to share a bed with Guinevere.'

She was off again, talking nonsense. How was he meant to answer that? Was this girl really for real? He couldn't think of anyone but Laurie who would have come out with that particular story at this juncture.

'No, I'll take the floor, thanks.'

'OK. Bagsy the bathroom first.'

The door shut and moments later he

heard the sound of the shower. He hung up their cagoules, sorted out his dry jeans and a T-shirt, then sat on the end of the bed and turned on the TV. Somehow it made him feel safer, almost as though there was another person in the room.

Not that he was scared of Laurie. Of course not. That would be ridiculous. All he knew was that right now he'd rather face Snake-tattoo with a flick-knife than Laurie with her talk of sharp swords.

He opened the wardrobe door. There were a couple of spare pillows in there and a blanket. Good. He'd be fine, absolutely fine — on the floor.

When some time later Laurie came out, she looked clean and fresh and smelled of something quite delicious. Her hair was still damp round the edges, and her brown mascara-free eyelashes were golden-tipped, he noticed. He tried not to stare. Somehow those golden tips made her eyes seem even more alluring.

Stop it, he told himself. *Just stop it.*

You have to be professional.

'Shall I make some more tea?' asked Laurie with another wicked smile. 'You won't be long in the shower, Toby, will you? Then we can watch the news together just like a cosy married couple.'

Speedily, Tom picked up his stuff and escaped into the calm of the bathroom. Once inside, he very deliberately locked the door. There were a couple of frillies residing on the radiator. He hardly spared them a glance. He'd shared a home with two sisters; he was used to seeing frillies about the place. It wasn't the frillies that bothered him. It was the never getting away from the temptation that was Laurie.

Keep it professional. Think of the advantages of the shared room — professionally speaking. On the whole it was a good thing. It made sense that he keep Laurie under close observation. To get to Laurie, Snake-tattoo would have to get through him first and, if they were sharing a room, well that would make that a whole lot more difficult for him.

All he had to do was convince Laurie.

Or was she already convinced? Was she not quite as bothered as she first made out? Maybe things like sharing a room with a complete stranger might not bother her one tiny iota. Maybe it was all part of her easy, laid-back lifestyle. Perhaps the initial outrage was just a token gesture. He'd play safe, keep quiet, sleep on the floor.

And tonight, while they ate, he'd take her through it all again. Every single little detail. There must be a reason, he argued to himself. There must be a reason Snake-tattoo was so dogged in finding Laurie. Somewhere in the back of her mind she must know something that would explain it.

On that thought, Tom's reflection, toothbrush poised to enter mouth, froze in the mirror before him as the idea dawned that maybe, just maybe, Laurie knew exactly what it was Snake-tattoo was after, didn't want to give it to him and was using Tom as protection. Perhaps she was in it up to her lovely neck. Perhaps she'd been in cahoots with Gemma all along and only when she'd found her friend's body abandoned in her flat had she realised that breaking the law could be a dirty, deadly business. She could have panicked and headed for the nearest police station with a wild, nearly true story.

Then she'd met Tom. Tom the patsy, as they said in American movies.

He clapped a hand to his head. What a dumb nut. Surely it couldn't be?

Slowly, he thought it through. The fear she'd expressed in the café, when she'd told him about spotting Snake-tattoo outside watching her flat, had been real enough. But how did he know what she'd been doing before they'd met over breakfast? Maybe she knew very well where the mystery missing object was hidden. Maybe it had indeed been in the camera case, the one she so conveniently suddenly discovered was missing. Maybe it wasn't missing at all and she'd stashed it away somewhere for the time being — possibly in her next-door neighbour's flat. What could be more convenient?

In that case the fear would have been real. When she saw Snake-tattoo was back she'd really freaked out and gone along with Tom's plans in order to protect herself. But things hadn't worked out, because it was becoming increasingly apparent that Snake-tattoo wasn't giving up. Hence the new, even sharper fear in her eyes.

Thoughtfully, Tom continued with his dental hygiene regime. Bang went his plan to take her to his mum and dad's place in Aldeburgh for safekeeping. That was no bad thing, though, because he'd only hit on the idea as a last resort.

He missed his family, and he owed them a visit, which he'd truly intended to make on this holiday. But one of the reasons he'd moved to London was in order to gain some privacy. He enjoyed seeing them, but only now and then, and when *he* did the choosing. Yes, although he loved his large, friendly family dearly, they shared one massive fault. They were to a man, or more often *woman*, nosy. Especially his sisters! He knew that if he took Laurie with him, although they'd welcome her with open arms, there would be questions. How would he handle those? Any hint of a female in Tom's life and they were on to it like bloodhounds, asking questions — personal, uncalled-for questions like what colour eyes did she have, how old was she, what was her figure like? Was she a smoker, how was her sense of humour, what perfume, how many brothers and sisters? The list went on and on.

But a wry smile twisted the corner of his mouth. The interrogation would not include, 'Does she go round killing her Australian mates, or is she a drug smuggler?' No, that would be too bizarre even for them to imagine.

So, hole up here for a while, well

away from the obvious route to her parents' home. Be cool. Go over everything again with Laurie, see if he could discover a flaw in her story, try to trip her up. He could do that. How hard could it be? So long as he didn't gaze for too long into those hypnotic tawny eyes of hers; so long as he didn't touch her, and experience again the magnetic pull she held for him.

Or perhaps not. A better, simpler strategy occurred to him. Soften her up. Let her imagine that she held him in thrall, totally under her spell. That wouldn't be too hard to pretend, would it? No, his heart went into overdrive at the very thought. She was tired, too; physically exhausted from the exertion of cycling, the rotten weather and the shock of her fall. Tired people became careless. Question her gently, keep her wine glass topped up. See what information he could garner. Spot things that didn't quite add up.

Pleased with himself for not giving in to any romantic notions about Laurie that might have been stealthily creeping up on him, Tom finished his ablutions. He hastily removed all traces of ever having being in the small, neat bathroom, apart from a toothbrush, deodorant and razor, and plunged back into the bedroom to find Laurie sitting crosslegged on the bed, a long piece of hair dangling sexily over one eye, studying his cycle tour map.

★　★　★

Laurie wasn't really looking at the map. She was wondering what exactly she'd done to get herself into such a muddle. It didn't help when Tom came hurtling out of the bathroom wearing a crumpled T-shirt and faded jeans, with tousled hair, dark, wet eyelashes and a wide smile. He smelled of clean male and toothpaste — a combination which suddenly seemed incredibly attractive.

'Crikey, you swatting up for the journey?'

'No, no, just looking to see how far to

Aldeburgh from here, although what looks like a simple, straight road on the map never is, is it? It's always full of twists and turns and takes forever.'

'Thought you liked seeing the countryside at a gentler pace?'

'I do. But not when I know Snake-tattoo could catch us up any moment in a Ferrari with a full arsenal of artillery in the boot.'

Tom snorted. 'That's extremely unlikely.'

'So you say. Anyway, I'm starving. Can we go and order dinner yet?'

'Not quite yet,' said Tom, looking at his watch. 'But we can go down for a drink. I think you could do with one after the shock you had earlier.'

She'd very nearly forgotten about the accident, but now he came to mention it, her hip was feeling a little bit bruised and her hands still smarted. Her rucksack hadn't dried out yet, so she just pocketed her purse and phone and followed Tom's broad back out of their room and down the twisting stairs to the bar.

'It's quite a maze in here,' she said. 'I bet the Americans love it. Quirky and quaint, and much bigger than it looks on the outside.'

'Well it's certainly popular,' said Tom. 'We only got this room because there was a cancellation.'

'Oh, that was lucky.' Lucky that there was a cancellation so that they didn't have to continue searching for another B&B in the pouring rain; unlucky in that they were now in the awkward position of one bed, two people.

But once they reached the bar, which was now half-full of customers, Laurie was able to put that out of her mind. They found a corner nook and Tom went to get the drinks while she studied her phone for any missed calls. One of her friends had texted 'Wot U up 2?' Laurie replied: 'Not a lot. Tell U 18r', hoping that she would indeed still be alive later in order to tell the tale!

Tom came back with two small tot glasses full of dark liquid, then went back for a couple of beers.

'What's that?' asked Laurie, eyeing the small glass suspiciously.

'Tot of rum and blackcurrant. It'll warm you up. You'll like it — trust me.'

Laurie took a tentative sip. It was smooth, it was warming; she liked it. She might even have another.

When they were eventually called to the dining area it turned out that the food on offer was more than simple pub food, but pub food at the top end of the market.

They settled in their seats and were given a menu each. 'This is my treat,' said Laurie suddenly. She held her hand up. 'Don't argue. You've been looking after me and I've been an ungrateful nuisance. This is your holiday and I've messed it up big-time.' Whatever was happening to her? She didn't usually do humble or grateful. She swallowed. 'I don't quite know how it's happened — the whole thing is utterly confusing — but one thing I do know is that without you, I'd have been well and truly . . . ' Without warning, her eyes filled with tears and she had to break off. Angrily, she pushed the tears away with the backs of her hands; it had to be the backs, as her palms were still stinging from her fall.

Shifting uncomfortably in his seat, Tom eyed her across the table. 'You haven't spoiled a thing,' he said gruffly. 'Quite enjoyed having you around, actually.'

'Oh . . . ' Laurie stared at him over the top of the menu she'd taken refuge behind. 'I haven't ruined it for you, then?'

'No.'

'You quite like me, then?'

Tom grinned. 'Oh, I wouldn't go so far as to say that.' He looked down at his menu then back up again, and for a long moment their eyes locked.

At first she thought she could see a hint of suspicion in his eyes, then suddenly he smiled and their expression changed to good-humoured affection. A few fireworks went off inside Laurie's head. She swallowed again. For a blinding moment she'd thought . . . Well, she didn't know what she'd thought. Something she'd no business to be thinking — especially when a few hours from now they were going to be sharing a room with only one bed in it.

Swiftly she collected herself and turned back to the menu, as though choosing what she was about to eat was the most engrossing pastime she'd ever experienced. Surreptitiously, she dabbed at her eyes with the paper napkin provided in the upright cutlery holder, and when she judged the silence to have gone on for long enough she said: 'I thought I'd try the scallops then go for the sea bass, but it all sounds good, doesn't it?' Good, her voice didn't sound shaky.

'I'm taken with the idea of the smoked salmon followed by the steak and ale pie.'

'Steak again? You had steak yesterday.'

'Anything wrong with that?'

'Nothing at all. It's your stomach, not mine.'

Once they'd placed their order, they sat quietly. The pub had filled up and the atmosphere was good. There was a lot of laughter being generated from one table of people in their early twenties, and a lovely family celebration was taking place at another. Laurie felt warm for the first time that day and although her body ached with tiredness, she didn't feel unhappy or tense, she realised. Instead, her mood was one of gentle contentment.

'This is nice,' she said before she could stop herself.

Tom glanced quickly at his surroundings. 'Yes; I've been here before. Thought you'd like it.'

Hastily, Laurie looked round again at the décor, not wanting him to realise that what she'd meant was nice was just the two of them together, sitting at a cosy table for two, out of the wind and the rain and, albeit momentarily, feeling safe.

Tom looked at her beer glass. 'Drink up. Don't want you to get dehydrated;

we haven't had much liquid today.'

Laurie raised her eyebrows.

'I'm not talking about the rain. That's on the outside. Trouble is, when it rains you don't feel thirsty and when you're cycling you really need to keep the fluids up.'

Ah, sweet. He really cared about her welfare. 'Can I just tell you, I only like beer when the weather's really hot,' she said. 'Can't you drink that for me? I'd rather have a glass of wine.'

'Done,' said Tom.

'I suppose a spritzer would be better?'

'No, you can always have another later if you're still thirsty.'

'OK.'

In the end a full bottle arrived at the table. Tom was right, she was thirsty, although she was quite sure she should really be drinking water, not wine. But Tom kept telling her to drink up because she deserved it, just like the shampoo ad. She wasn't sure she did, but it was nice that someone thought she deserved something pleasant for a change.

The scallops were lovely, with just enough garlic, and the sea bass even better. For a while apart from the odd *mmm* of appreciation, conversation was at a minimum. Then Tom took it into his head to start questioning her about the day before yesterday, all the events in chronological order and exactly what she did at what time and when. And, oh dear, she was just too tired for this.

By now she was on her third glass of wine and yawning widely. 'Sorry, Tom,' she said. 'I know you're a policeman and all that, but I just can't go through it all again. I've told you everything I know, and I can hardly keep my eyes open.'

'OK,' said Tom. 'Let's go and sit at the more comfortable seats in the bar and free this table up for someone else. Can't go to bed yet; far too early.'

Laurie thought otherwise. Surely she could go on up and he could come up later and sleep on the floor. What was wrong with that? Then she caught sight of him smothering a yawn and realised that he was probably tired too, with all the stuff they'd done that day. Good! So long as he didn't snore too loudly.

When she got to her feet, she acknowledged that a combination of tiredness, a tot of rum and three glasses of wine — and they were large glasses, she recognised in retrospect — seemed to have affected her ability to walk.

'Oh dear,' she said, 'oh, so sorry,' as she bashed into a table.

Grinning, Tom took her arm. 'Come on, sit down for a bit. I'll get you some water.'

'This isn't like me,' she went on once she was sitting again on an upholstered seat in a small nook Tom had guided her to. 'I hate being out of control. Not my thing at all.'

'It's probably delayed shock.'

'Nonsense. It's three glasses of wine, is what it is. I'll have that water, please, or I won't be able to ride my bike straight in the morning.'

The nook Tom had found was quieter and much more private. Laurie rested her head against the back of the seat.

'So, tell me about you,' she said. 'Tell me about your family. I'm an only child; I'd have loved to have had brothers and sisters.

'Two-edged sword,' said Tom. 'Lack of privacy. My sisters, especially, always have to *know* everything. I had to share my bedroom too. No, not with my sisters, with my younger brother; and he used to sleepwalk and talk. Also borrow my things and not put them back. Anyway, now I've gone and my oldest sister — she's married now and has twins — he's got the room to himself and my mum's got her study and the spare room back.'

'You must have a big house.'

Tom pulled a face. 'Not big enough. There's five of us kids, Mum and Dad, and an assortment of animals. My dad has to have an office at home — he's a builder. My mum needs an office, really — she does party planning or some such thing. We really need a little room where we can shut the door to be private — so that's the conservatory. The rest of the house is open-plan. Kitchen, dining room, sitting room, hall — no hiding place!'

'Must have been fun though — when you were young.'

'Yeah, I suppose it was . . . Nice to have some private space though.' He paused, then looked at her searchingly. 'Anyway, what am I doing banging on about me? Let's get back to you. Is that why you went to South Africa, to get some space?'

Laurie sat up straight. 'No, I told you. I went to be with my boyfriend. I went as his assistant. I was a good one too. Did all the admin, all the organising. All the tough jobs; dealing with difficult people. I checked the equipment, got the lighting sorted out. Shame he turned out to be a lazy, ungrateful boss, full of himself and his own ego.' She shrugged her shoulders. 'Took me a while to realise I was being used, and even longer to realise I was being two-timed, too. Oh well, you win some, you lose some.' She stopped as suddenly as she'd started.

Why was she telling him all this?

Wearily, she sank back against the tapestry pub seat. She'd relaxed too much, that was why. What with the wine, the warmth of the pub, the good food inside her, Tom's sympathetic but sudden questioning, it had all come out in a rush.

'I think I'm ready for my bed,' she said. 'I'm really tired.'

'OK,' said Tom. 'You go on up. Get yourself sorted out. I'll be up in about twenty minutes. There's extra bedding in the cupboard; I'll sleep on the floor.'

Haltingly, Laurie got to her feet. Things were looking a trifle indistinct, a bit blurred and tilted. 'I tell you what,' she said in a voice that slurred slightly. 'I don't quite honestly think I can find my way back to the room.'

'Right.' Tom finished his last inch of beer. 'Come on, then. I'll help you, you poor old lady.'

'Thank you, Toby.' Even to her own ears, her laugh sounded slightly out of control. 'When you've lost your way — ask a policeman.'

Tom grinned. 'Not in this day and age. You'd be lucky to find one.'

'I must have got lucky then.'

The swing door looked to be about a mile away. Still giggling to herself, she walked carefully towards it and negotiated it without a problem. But the stairs were a different matter.

'Lotsh of stairs,' she said. 'Lotsh more than there were.'

Tom said nothing; just kept his hands firmly on her waist and guided her upwards.

'That's nice,' she said. 'Has anyone ever told you, you have nice hands?'

'All the time,' said Tom. 'It's the hand cream I use.'

Laurie collapsed into giggles again. 'That's so funny,' she gasped. 'You're so dry. You just kill me.'

'Come on,' said Tom, heaving her through a fire door. 'We're nearly there.'

'Nearly there, nearly there,' sang Laurie.

She felt him prop her up against the wall while he fumbled for the key. She felt herself slide down it, and that also seemed to be incredibly funny. 'Can't seem to shtand up,' she said.

Tom grasped her under her armpits and hauled her to her feet, then gazed at her intently.

'What?' she said, and smiled to take the rudeness out of the question.

His face was very close to hers and he was still looking into her eyes. 'I'm wondering what you're thinking?'

'Eashy. About how it would feel to kiss you.'

'What?'

'Well, don't tell me you haven't thought about it.'

'Of course I have. I'm a bloke.'

'Well, you haven't done anything about it.'

'No.'

'Why not?'

'I wouldn't be comfortable with it.'

'Oh.'

'Or maybe I'd be too comfortable with it.'

Laurie tried in vain to read his expression. 'Then we'd be in trouble,' she said eventually.

'You're probably right.'

The door was opened and she was dumped on the bed without ceremony. Vaguely she felt him removing her shoes, putting her head on the pillow and dragging her legs into a stretched-out position on the bed.

'Tom,' she said, groping for a pillow and placing it next to her. 'Lancelot's sword. You can't sleep on the floor. The bed's huge. I promise I won't ravish you in the night. Jusht leave the pillow there; we'll be fine.'

Then she must have gone to sleep and started dreaming immediately, because she thought she heard him say: 'You're a sweet girl, Laurie, d'you know that?'

But that couldn't be true. So she must have been dreaming, mustn't she?

Tom looked down at Laurie's peaceful face. Her cheeks were slightly flushed, her mouth closed but relaxed. The lips looked very inviting. Tenderly, he turned her onto her side and eased the duvet over her, gently tucking her hands underneath. They were slim hands with square, unvarnished nails that were cut short, but not too short. When he'd removed her shoes he'd seen that her toenails were painted blue.

Staring at her, he wondered just why it was that this girl, this particular girl, with her yellow eyes and blue toenails, seemed to possess the ability to make him feel helpless yet protective, angry but happy all at the same time. He was experiencing feelings he'd never had before, and yet . . . and yet . . .

Get a hold of yourself, DI Jessop. This is not the way to interrogate a suspect.

But *was* she a suspect? And if she was, what was he going to do about it?

There was a chair in the corner of the room. Wearily he lowered himself into it. The sensible thing to do would be to get back to being a policeman. Run the whole scenario past someone else. A professional person. Someone unbiased. Someone who hadn't allowed his judgement to become clouded by totally inappropriate feelings.

He heaved a sigh. The facts hadn't altered. No body, no crime. Just a scared girl. No, a scared, beautiful girl with either a strong imagination, or a very real reason to be scared. Whether by accident or design, Laurie was very much a part of this horrible mess; and whatever the truth was, Tom was in it too, right up to his neck. And that didn't include a bypass round the region of his heart. He was uncomfortably aware that it was also well and truly engaged.

He put his head in his hands and groaned.

8

When Laurie first stirred she had difficulty remembering where she was, what day it was, and even *who* she was.

When she did remember, she wished she hadn't.

Cautiously she opened one eye. It didn't hurt quite so much as she'd imagined, so she opened the other and registered the fact that the pillow was still lengthwise next to her — and Tom wasn't. She groaned softly to herself. Was that good or bad?

She'd been seriously squiffy last night. What on earth would he think of her? But then again, so what? After all, she'd only known him what, two days? Three?

A hundred years?

Why should she care where he was, or what he thought?

But where was he, and what did he think?

All she could remember was that somewhere along the line he'd suddenly changed back from attractive dinner companion to policeman and started questioning her to within an inch of her life, and she hadn't liked it. Then she remembered the ever-so-nearly-kissing moment. She closed her eyes as though in pain and turned her head to the pillow to save herself from embarrassment. Yes, they nearly had — but then they hadn't.

What a good job that was.

Kisses would make a complicated, uncomfortable situation even more so.

Even so . . . For a moment she gave herself up to imagining just what it might feel like. His soft yet firm mouth landing on hers, his tongue maybe exploring a little. The feel of his arms around her, her fingers straying into the crisp, dark hair at the base of his skull, then lingering there as she responded to his kiss.

Stop it. Just stop it.

Realising with relief that she was still

fully clothed, Laurie pushed the duvet back and gingerly made her way to the bathroom. His toothbrush was still there, but his towel was damp. He must be waiting for her downstairs, so she'd better hurry.

She groaned. She had a feeling today would be a long one.

Sure enough, by the time she reached the dining room and located Tom, she found that he'd already devoured half the bacon and eggs on his plate.

Briefly, he glanced up and raised his eyebrows at her. 'Good morning, Lulu. Your breakfast's on its way.'

'Right.' Laurie eyed his plate dubiously. She wasn't sure she could cope with the egg yolk and the way it was mingling with the ketchup.

'Go on, you'll feel a whole lot better when you're on the outside of a good meal.'

'Right,' said Laurie again, aware that she was sounding like a scratched CD.

A smiling waitress deposited a plate in front of her and exchanged a knowing wink with Tom. 'Your other half said you wouldn't be long,' she said. 'Enjoy.'

'R-really?' Thank goodness she'd managed to find another word that started with 'r' apart from 'right'. 'Thanks.'

Tom was correct, though, she thought some fifteen minutes later. A good hot breakfast, tea and toast, and two cups of tea further on, she did feel more like a human being again.

'Well, did I snore?' Tom gave an enigmatic smile.

'Well, did I?'

'Like a rhinoceros.'

'I didn't!'

'All right.' He gave another smile.

'You're not meant to tell a girl she snores like a rhinoceros!'

'OK. A lady racehorse then.'

'When have we got to leave?' she asked after a long silence. It was the first time she'd looked at him directly today and oh yes, he was still as fanciable as yesterday. Drat. Why couldn't he have grown repellent overnight?

Tom gave her a cool, appraising glance. 'We're not leaving. Not today anyway. We're going to hole up here and go over every little thing again and you're going to tell me everything.'

Oh no, not again. She didn't have the strength for this, she really didn't. 'B-but I've already told you everything. You know I have.' It sounded pathetic, even to her own ears.

A sudden ruthless gleam appeared in his eyes as he leaned forward. Suddenly it was easy to imagine that it wouldn't be a very comfortable experience to be held in custody and interrogated by DI Jessop.

'I mean everything,' Tom repeated. 'And if there *was* anything in your 'suddenly missing' camera case that you knew about, you'd better let me in on that little secret too.'

A surge of sudden anger welled up inside her. How dare he speak to her like this? Before she knew it, she was leaning forward too and they were glaring at each other, head to head, over the top of the cutlery holder, the tea pot and the tomato ketchup bottle. 'Listen, Mr Plod,' she said through clenched teeth, 'I'm about fed up with your insinuations. I've told you everything I know, you know I have. Why should I stay here with you and let you put me through all this?' She took a deep breath and leaned back again. 'Tell you what. I'm going to go upstairs, pack my stuff, phone my mum and she'll come and pick me up. We've got locks on our doors. We'll wait till my dad comes home — he'll know what to do — and at least he'll believe me. I don't need this — not any of it.' Laurie pushed her chair back and exited the dining room with and her chin at a slightly sharper angle than usual, and a heightened colour in her cheeks.

How dare he? she thought. What a nerve. And here she was, thinking they'd got over all that. Why would he suddenly revert to disbelieving her again? Angrily she pushed away a sudden tear that was trickling down her hot cheek. Turning to go up the stairs and back to their room, she caught a glimpse of the dining room through the swing door. Tom was dropping his napkin onto his plate and getting to his feet as though to follow her.

As soon as the swing door was safely shut she turned in the opposite direction and pushed through the front entrance. Fresh air, that was what she needed. By the time Tom had chased upstairs looking for her, no doubt in order to bully her some more, she'd be down the road and out of sight, giving herself a chance to cool off.

But what would Tom be doing? Would he be cooling off too, or would he have something else on the agenda before racing after her in order to cause more aggravation? Calling one of his copper buddies, for instance?

Looking around, Laurie took a moment to recognise that it was a lovely day. She turned left down the road, noting that there was a twist that would take her out of sight quite quickly. After all, she didn't know how long Tom's call to his copper buddy might take.

Or maybe the call wouldn't be to a copper buddy, always assuming he had any buddies who weren't coppers of course. Huh, if he went round bullying people in the way he bullied her, he probably didn't have any friends at all, coppers or not.

Just a minute. Although her pace didn't falter, Laurie hung on to that thought. Just who *were* his buddies?

He didn't believe her, did he? So why on earth should she believe him?

Brain working furiously, Laurie strode on up the road. The twist in the road turned out to be a nasty fork. A car was approaching from the right. Automatically, she stepped in closer to the hedge. There was a glimpse of a shaved head and a black T-shirt. In the habit of doing a double-take with every shaved head she spied, Laurie had to force herself not to turn her head and stare after the car. She'd only ever seen him in a white T-shirt before but, she reasoned, even

Snake-tattoo would change his T-shirt now and then. A shudder overtook her and her heart started on a fast tango. Could it have been Snake-tattoo? But the car carried on towards the pub, and the driver had surely hardly spared her a glance. The sun had been too bright, the interior of the car too shady for her make out any features.

Decisively she continued up the road. Of course it wasn't Snake-tattoo; he was probably parked up within view of the Kendal residence, watching her mother loading the car with theatrical gear before setting off for rehearsals. She really must get a grip.

Her pace increased to a smart one which matched her thoughts.

But, thinking of Snake-tattoo . . . Suppose this was all a charade? Suppose Tom had plenty of *criminals* for buddies. *Suppose he was in league with Snake-tattoo?*

But that was ridiculous — wasn't it?

She caught her breath at the idea and examined it some more. It wasn't unheard-of for a policeman to be a baddie. What did they say on the telly? 'On the take', that was it. Suppose Tom was on the take and had tried the soft approach to start with to see if she knew more than she was letting on. After all, how did she know Snake-tattoo hadn't spotted her in the café and phoned Tom to chat her up and find out a bit more? Suppose he and Snake-tattoo knew exactly what they were looking for, but just couldn't find it and had come to the conclusion she'd stashed it somewhere other than the flat. What better scenario than to keep one of them, disguised as a friend and confidant, with her, the other following as some just-out-of-focus threat. The combination should be enough to break her and make her spill everything she knew.

The only problem was, even if they broke her, she didn't *know* anything, either consciously or subconsciously.

A feeling of despair engulfed her. If she couldn't trust Tom, what on earth was she going to do?

Entirely uninvited, a vision of his intense gaze came into her mind. She recalled the way he'd gently helped her up after her spill from her bike; his look of concern which belied his rallying tone that of course she was fine and it was only two more miles. He could be kind, he could be gentle. She'd ruined his holiday, yet he was still trying to do his best to help her.

Purposefully, Laurie lengthened her stride. The whole thing was crazy. *Of course* Tom wasn't a bent copper; just an extremely annoying one.

Thank goodness she'd only had her purse on her when she'd come down to breakfast. She'd even left her phone in her room. If she'd had her phone with her she might have been tempted to call her mother straight away, and that would have been a disaster. Imagining the wobbly her mother would have thrown, she shut her eyes briefly. No, she had to face it. Just for the moment, she was stuck with Tom. She'd just have to make the best of it and convince him, all over again, that she was telling the truth.

There was a general store up ahead with a newspaper stand set outside.

Right, OK. Simmer down. Buy a newspaper, then go back to the pub and well, not eat humble pie exactly, but at least have the good grace to make an apology — even if he doesn't deserve one.

★ ★ ★

Well, Tom, you made a great job of that, didn't you just?

Although her things were still there, the bike panniers neatly packed, her rucksack standing unfastened on the bed, their room was empty of Laurie. He'd already booked it for another night, so once again he'd be playing Lancelot. Always provided Laurie stuck around long enough. Thank goodness that by Saturday Laurie's father would be home and Tom could justifiably take her back to where she belonged with two responsible parents to look out for her. He was no good at being nursemaid — especially not to someone as infuriating and as beautiful as Laurie. Especially when he'd allowed himself to become so attracted to her.

He left their room for the chambermaid to sort out and slowly made his way back downstairs. He went outside and looked both ways at the empty winding road. Obviously Laurie must have stormed off somewhere, and the road had so many twists and turns she could have gone in either direction. Tom decided to play a waiting game and stationed himself in the annex near the pub entrance where he could keep an eye on all comings and goings. He took his map out of his back pocket and examined it. Perhaps when she'd calmed down a bit they could go for a walk. A pleasant, country stroll. The weather looked set to be fair. They could just walk and talk, and enjoy getting to know one another in the way they would have done had they met at a party, say.

He smiled to himself. Who was he kidding? Their paths would never have crossed at a party. Tom didn't go to parties made up of photographers, models, and media folk. Rugby players, fellow police and hairdressers were more his style. In the normal way of things Laurie and he would never, ever have met.

And that would have been a terrible shame, he realised with a jolt.

He looked at his watch. Where was she?

Should he get his bike and go looking for her? What if Snake-tattoo was out there and happened to come across her? She wouldn't stand a chance. On a country road she could be bundled into a car in a trice.

Tom went hot and cold at the thought, jerked to his feet and, not even stopping to fetch his cycle helmet, strode out to fetch his bike from round the back of the pub, narrowly avoiding a car that had just turned off the road in the process.

He sighed with relief when after negotiating the first bend and choosing the right fork, he could just make her out walking towards him with a newspaper under her arm. Slowly he headed towards her, turned his bike in a circle without looking at her and slowed down his pace to match hers before snatching a sidelong peek. Her face was pink and she glanced at him from under lowered lids.

'Sorry. I lost it a bit,' she mumbled.

'Not your fault,' said Tom. 'I'm not used to interviewing someone I care about. It's hard to be impersonal.'

Cared about? What had he said?

There was a long silence. 'You were that all right,' she said, ignoring the earlier comment about 'caring'. 'You were impersonal personified.'

Tom dismounted and wheeled his bike alongside her. 'Did you phone your mum?'

'Left it in the room.'

Relief tided over him. They had a bit longer then. Even sparring with her was better than nothing.

She gave a half-laugh.

'What's funny?'

'Everything. Just now, I was even thinking you were a bent copper.'

'What?'

'Yes. Mad or what? But you get bent coppers, don't you? I thought you were trying to soften me up. You know — being nice to me. Well, you were a bit nice yesterday. Not so much today though. So come on, be straight with me. You never did completely believe me, did you?' Tom frowned while searching for an answer. But Laurie didn't want to wait. 'You didn't, did you? Even right at the beginning, when I came to the police station, why didn't you believe me then?'

Tom sighed. 'You were too calm. We — I — thought you were acting a part.'

'Well I was, I was acting a part. Of course I was. I was acting the part of a calm woman. Inside I was far from calm, believe me. Inside I was having the heebie jeebies.'

'The heebie jeebies?'

'And some. I thought if I let you see how hysterical I felt, you'd think I was nuts. But it turns out you thought I was nuts anyway. Either that, or a master criminal.' A giggle escaped her. 'An arms dealer? Do me a favour. Smuggling guns? In a camera case?' She gave a snort. 'Never heard anything so mad. I thought the police were meant to be clever!'

Tom didn't like the way this was going. The last thing he wanted was to enter another argument with Laurie, but he couldn't let that one go.

'Try looking at it from my perspective for a moment. Suppose I believe every word you say. You must either have or be hiding something, or why so much interest in you? I mean, what have I actually got to go on, in terms of concrete facts? One-sided phone conversations that you repeat to me about Snake-tattoo, who is hunting you down by phone? I've had no sightings of this guy, no phone conversations with him, and I don't know anyone else who has.

There was no dead body. Nothing. Doesn't leave me with a great deal to go on other than complete trust in you, does it?'

Laurie blinked in surprise, then drew those well-marked eyebrows of hers together. Tom took a step back at the ferocity of her glare. 'Well listen here, friend,' she spat out. 'From my point of view there wasn't a lot to trust you about either. Bit of a coincidence wasn't it? You being on holiday, happening to be going in my direction? Having a 'spare' bike? Suddenly being nice to me? Pretending to believe me? If it wasn't so ridiculous, how do I know you're not one of Snake-tattoo's gang?'

They'd stopped walking by this time and were standing facing each other with Tom's bike between them. He could see the fury still in Laurie's eyes. But mixed up with the fury was another expression which with a qualm he recognised as hurt.

For a long moment they stared at each other.

There was the shrill sound of his mobile phone. He ignored it. Now was not the time.

Laurie gave a shaky smile. 'Basically, you still don't trust me, do you?'

'I would do, if you trusted me.'

'Huh. You're so right. Why should *I* trust you?'

She was so beautiful, and so totally unaware of the effect she was having on him. Tom nearly burst at the injustice of it all. 'How can you ask that when I've been with you twenty-four seven for the last few days and never even touched you?'

'What's that got to do with anything?'

Tom lifted his hand and traced a finger down her cheek. 'It's got everything to do with everything,' he said softly. 'Why am I here with you? Risking my career for you? You could be in league with drug smugglers; you could be a crazy woman who needs locking up. But I'm still here with you, right?'

Laurie turned and started walking on

towards the pub. 'I think I'd best make that call to my mum, and leave you to get on with your life,' she threw over her shoulder.

Miserably, Tom watched her go. Get on with his life? Life without Laurie? Suddenly the idea seemed impossible.

Should he get on his bike, catch her up? Or head off in the opposite direction; get up a bit of speed? Do what he'd planned to do — enjoy the open road? Do the sensible thing: put all ideas of this mad girl with the serious eyebrows right out of his mind once and for all?

Oh well, best just attend to his missed call first.

★　★　★

After walking twenty paces and hearing no sound of Tom following her, Laurie risked a quick glance over her shoulder. Head bent, he was concentrating on his phone. Quickly, she turned her eyes to the front and ignoring the hammering of her heart, continued walking briskly up the road. It wasn't far to the pub now. She didn't know what she'd do when she got there, but anything was better than standing rowing with Tom in the middle of the street while wishing all the time that they could stop talking for a moment and that he would take her in his arms and kiss her completely stupid.

And suddenly he was there. She heard the whoosh of his bike tyres and he was next to her smiling that lopsided smile of his. 'Sorry,' he said, dismounting. 'This isn't the time for arguments. Let's forgive each other, get back to the pub and decide what to do with the day. I've had a message from PC Morgan to ring the station. I just phoned back but she's not answering at the moment.'

'Don't they even leave you alone when you're on holiday?' she asked after a pause, during which time she tried to quell her relief that he hadn't quite washed his hands of her yet.

'Usually, yes. It must be important.'

Laurie wondered what it must be like to have a job where you were almost indispensable. Not that she was impressed by that. Not at all. But she glanced at him sideways with a new respect in her eyes.

When they got back to the pub they went straight to reception intending to arrange for another night's stay. 'I was going to try to book you a separate room,' he said apologetically. 'But then I thought that negotiating corridors or whatever in order to keep an eye on you would be stupid, so I'll have to play Lancelot again I'm afraid.'

Thinking of her panic at the glimpse of a shaven-haired driver not too long ago, Laurie said nothing. She was an adult; they both were. Surely they could cope with sharing a room without becoming overly dramatic about it?

They arrived at the deserted desk. The guest book was open and the room keys were positioned on hooks on the wall behind.

'Perhaps you should ring the bell,' suggested Laurie, for whom patience had never been a virtue.

'Hi there. Sorry to keep you.' The friendly receptionist from yesterday bustled in and squeezed her ample frame behind the desk. She looked at them curiously. 'There was a guy looking for you earlier.'

An icy fear griped Laurie's stomach. 'What did he look like?'

'Tallish, built like a boxer. Shaved head.'

She took a moment to digest this. 'Right. I don't suppose you happened to notice if he had a tattoo on the back of his neck?'

'Yes, actually I did. Couldn't tell you what it was, though. Very nosey, I thought, the way he was asking about you. I wondered if he was an ex-boyfriend or something?'

Please! Credit me with some taste, thought Laurie in spite of her fast-creeping terror.

'He said he was a friend of yours and

237

wanted to surprise you. Said your name was Laurie . . . Lulu's a pet name I take it?' She nodded in Tom's direction. 'Didn't mention *you*, not by name anyway.'

'Has he booked in?' asked Tom.

'What did you tell him?' said Laurie at the same time.

'That was the funny thing — he didn't book in. I thought he'd left, but about five minutes later I saw him come down the stairs and before I could get out from behind here — ' She indicated the desk. ' — and ask what the hell he was doing, he'd gone! I shouldn't worry though. I didn't tell him anything. Not that there was anything to tell. He gave me your description, said you were on bikes, so of course I knew immediately you were here. He wanted to know what room you were in, but I didn't tell him. I don't know why, but I didn't trust him somehow.'

'Right,' said Tom grimly. 'Thanks, but we'll check anyway.'

They made their way to their room

quickly and in silence.

The door did not appear to have been tampered with and was still locked. As they looked round the room Laurie gave a sigh of relief. 'Nothing's been disturbed,' she said. 'Look, my phone's over there, the panniers are where I left them, and so's my rucksack. I had my purse and my cards in my pocket anyway, so that's all right. But what is this guy playing at?'

Tom frowned. 'I have to admit, I have absolutely no idea,' he said. 'He's been in this room though, I can feel it. The guest book just lies on the counter; anyone could see it. I'll even bet he nicked a spare key off the hook ... I think we should get out of here.'

'Suits me. But he might not have got in,' said Laurie hopefully. 'You're not infallible, my dear Sherlock. But if he *did* get in, had a poke around and didn't take anything, that means ...That means he's still looking for *me* — isn't he? He thinks I know something. Oh God. I don't. I don't!'

'We'll put our bikes on the train and get back to London,' said Tom. 'We've got everything ready. We'll go straight away.'

'Right,' said Laurie, reaching for her rucksack.

A sudden shrill ringtone made them both jump.

'It's mine,' said Tom, fishing in his pocket for his mobile. 'Hi, Jude! What's up?' His eyebrows raised a notch. 'Really? Where? How long ago? No, right! Look, I'll have to call you back. Keep me informed, would you, Jude?' He slipped his phone back in his pocket.

'What?' said Laurie. 'Why are you looking at me like that?'

'Sit down,' ordered Tom. Something about his tone made her obey.

'They've found a body that answers your friend's description. She was wrapped in a rug, dumped in a skip, and her neck was broken. They're looking for you now, but you don't seem to be at your flat and they haven't been able to get hold of your mother yet to see if you're there. They want you to identify the body.'

9

'If they phone my mother, she'll go completely nuts,' said Laurie. 'She's not in amateur dramatics for nothing.' Her voice, Tom noticed, was slightly wobbly. 'What should we do next?'

'While we're here we're safe,' he said in what he hoped was a reassuring tone. 'This is a busy pub; he's not going to come charging in here again.'

Laurie's eyebrows drew together and she took in a sudden shaky breath. 'Oh dear, I've just thought — I didn't tell you, did I? I thought I saw him out on the road.'

Tom's reassuring manner vanished in a trice. 'What? Bit late to tell me now, isn't it? Why on earth didn't you say earlier?'

Her eyes sparked dangerously. 'Oh, and have you accusing me of being a mad woman again?'

That was fair, he supposed, but the knowledge didn't make him any less cross. 'Well, did he see you? What?'

'No, I'm sure he didn't. He was driving towards the pub and I suppose if he was looking for anything, it would have been two cyclists, one with long blond hair. Actually, the sun was in my eyes and I wasn't even completely sure it was him, but now we know he's been here . . . Well . . . In retrospect I'm pretty sure it was.'

Tom sighed. 'Well, even if it was, at least we also know that Gemma's been found.'

'True, that's a little ray of sunshine for us to take comfort from. Not so much poor Gemma though.' She gave him a discerning glance. 'And at least having confirmation from the receptionist that Snake-tattoo isn't a figment of my imagination has stopped you looking at me as though you'd like to strangle me.'

'I never did that,' said Tom hotly. 'Did I?'

'You did. Especially this morning.

This morning it was daggers drawn. I was quite frightened. You had an expression that would have done credit to an axe murderer — at the very least.'

'I've never looked at you as though I was an axe murderer.' He smiled. 'Anyway, how d'you know I'm not?'

'You're a policeman and besides, you haven't got an axe.' Her eyes widened. 'Have you?'

'Very funny.' Oh Lord, he supposed an apology was called for. He cleared his throat.

'I'm sorry if I upset you. I was just a bit anxious.' Laurie just hugged her rucksack closer to her body and didn't reply. He cleared his throat again. 'Anyway, we have to decide what we do next. Any ideas?'

'Have you told them at the office — I mean station — that I'm with you?'

Tom hoped he didn't look as sheep-ish as he felt. 'Not yet. But I should, really.' *Yep, DI Jessop, how are you going to explain that one away?* he asked himself. Thoughtfully, he watched as Laurie

244

bent over her rucksack, her hair falling forward to expose an area of pale skin at the back of her neck. It looked soft and vulnerable. He thought he'd like to kiss her, right there on the back of her neck, or anywhere else really.

She readjusted the rucksack on her lap. Then, as she fingered the bottom of the bag, Tom saw her expression change. 'Hang on a minute,' she said, turning it on its side and inspecting the lower seam closely. 'This isn't mine!'

It took a moment for him to comprehend her meaning. 'What d'you mean, it isn't yours?'

'It isn't mine! Mine had that bit of unpicked seam at the bottom here, don't you remember? I showed you.'

'Check what's in there,' said Tom at exactly the same time as Laurie started emptying the contents on the bed.

'Just a sweater, some chocolate, wet wipes, small make-up bag, tissues, flat keys, notebook and pen . . . Only stuff I need and don't want to leave unattended in my panniers, in case we stop off for a drink or something. All I've got in the panniers is dirty washing in one and a few clean clothes and my wash bag in the other. That's it. I travel light.'

She certainly did, compared to most of the other girls of his acquaintance, thought Tom in admiration. 'So . . . ' he said slowly. 'He's been here, we know that. Your rucksack appears to have changed.' He clapped his hand to his forehead. '*Of course*, dumb cluck that I am, it must have been the rucksack he wanted all along . . . *Your* rucksack, not Gemma's. He must have taken hers from your flat when he killed her, thinking she was you. He took the only rucksack that was there, which he assumed belonged to you, and now he's switched them back.'

Slowly Tom sat down on the bed. 'But why? Why on earth? What's to want about it? What was different about it?' He peered inside and searched with his fingers. There was nothing there. Of course, there wouldn't be. 'Hang on. When you mended the one he's taken

— you said you mended it, didn't you, when you realised the stitching had come undone?'

'Yeah, well after a fashion. Needle-work's never been one of my strengths, only enough to make it safe and respectable.'

'Was there anything in there? In the enclosed bit of seam at the bottom?'

She gave a wobbly grin. 'What, like weapons of mass destruction, d'you mean? No, of course there wasn't anything in there. Only little bags of silicon, you know to keep the inside dry. You get them in all bags when they're new.'

'Oh,' said Tom in disappointment. 'No packets of white powder, tiny memory cards or anything like that?' he went on hopefully.

'No, nothing. No neat little packets of cocaine or heroin — not that I'd know the difference. No microchips containing classified information. Nothing. Zilch! Only the silicon bags, and they'd split anyway. I took them out;

they were knobbly and uncomfortable.' Suddenly a grin came across her face. 'Hey, you know what this means?' she said, giving him a sudden punch on the arm. 'He's got the rucksack now, so who cares why he wanted it? He's carefully and thoughtfully changed it for the other one; probably doesn't even think I'd notice. He's going to leave me alone now, isn't he?'

She sat on the bed amidst the contents of the rucksack, a wide smile of relief spreading across her face, and all Tom could think of for a wild moment was once again how much he wanted to kiss her.

'I'm free of him, aren't I?' she went on. 'Why would he worry about me now?'

Something other than kissing her was now niggling away at the back of Tom's mind, but he forced an answering grin. 'I suppose so . . . ' *Get real, Tom. Get back to reality*. 'But we've still got to get you back as soon as possible. You've got a body to identify.'

Her face dropped a little. 'Oh yes, I suppose I'll have to do that, won't I?' She started to gather her things together, then stopped as another thought struck her. 'Tom? The police will believe me now, won't they? They'll have to.' Her face paled. 'They won't think . . . they won't think *I've* done it, will they? They won't think I killed Gemma, wrapped her in my rug, dumped her in a skip, then reported her missing? They can't possibly think that, can they?'

Tom swallowed. 'Well, they'll have to interview you — obviously they'll have to do that.'

'Obviously,' repeated Laurie in a dull voice.

'Look, don't worry. They'll find out what time she died, well, approximately. You were at work all morning and went straight home. Once you'd found the body you reported it — perfectly the proper thing to do.'

'Huh,' said Laurie. 'You didn't say that at the time.'

'They'll do a sort of timeline, and all the times will pan out, making it impossible for you to have done even half of that, always assuming you had the strength,' went on, Tom ignoring the interruption. 'Carting a body around is hard work, you know. And you've got no car. How would you get a body down the stairs, for a start? And after that, out of the area and into a skip, all completely unnoticed?' His voice petered out. He wasn't sure from Laurie's expression whether he was making things better or worse.

She didn't say anything, just fixed him with her tawny eyes and gave a sigh.

'We'd better get going then. No more Lancelot and Guinevere tonight,' he said after a moment longer. 'We'll go down, tell reception nothing's missing and pay the bill. Then we'll make tracks. I don't think the station's too far away. I'll check the train for Chelmsford, then London for the quickest way back home. I reckon Snake-tattoo will be long gone . . . Yes,' he repeated.

'Now he's got what he wanted he'll be well away. Strange, though . . . really, really strange. I mean, what could it be? Why?'

★ ★ ★

Laurie was still curious. She was only human, after all, and there were lots of unanswered questions mainly beginning with the word 'why'. None of it made any sense as far as she could see. But so what? She was free. No more looking over her shoulder worrying whether or not a knife would be slid between her ribs. Whatever it was that Gemma had been involved in had absolutely nothing to do with her. If Snake-tattoo had a fetish about owning her rucksack in the same way as other odd people went about collecting shoes, that was fine with her as long as that was all he was after. And it must be, she told herself, otherwise how could they now be cycling along the country roads towards the railway station without a car having passed them for miles? It was a little bit weird that he had known they were on bikes, but then she remembered that Tom had confided in Pilar about the cycling holiday. He was obviously smart enough to have made the connection and, as Tom had said, was sweeping the area in order to find them. He'd just been much quicker than they'd thought he'd be in catching up with them. Snake-tattoo, despite his tasteless tattoo, was obviously a smart operator.

Although she was still a little concerned at the prospect of the interview with the police, there was no reason for her to feel frightened anymore, was there?

Then, even though she'd promised herself she wouldn't, she looked over her shoulder. No, only a couple of lorries and another batch of cyclists in the distance. Lovely.

Ahead of her Tom was indicating that he was slowing down and turning left. Good job one of them knew where they were going. She didn't have a clue where they were.

'Soon be time for coffee,' said Tom when she'd caught up with him. 'There's a café on this road which also leads to the station. You deserve it. You haven't moaned once about being thirsty.'

'Well, I've had my water. Wait a minute.' She narrowed her eyes suspiciously. 'Why are you being nice to me?'

'I keep telling you, I *am* nice. Just because I'm a policeman doesn't mean I'm not nice.'

Laurie narrowed her eyes still further. 'I know why you're being nice. You don't want me to tell your colleagues that we had to share a room, do you? You've got rules about that sort of thing. You know, 'thou must not share a room with a police suspect'? Something like that?'

'You were never a police suspect, Laurie. Don't be ridiculous.'

'No, but I might be now.'

'I won't even be on your case. Not unless I cut my holiday short. I was meant to be having the whole week.'

'Oh yes, I'd forgotten,' said Laurie in

a subdued voice.

After about half a mile's cycling on a very minor road they came to a shop which sold touristy bits and pieces: locally made honey, eggs, coasters with scenes of various country landmarks; and it also had a couple of tables out front where coffee was served.

Laurie left Tom studying his map on the small rickety table and went to order the coffees. It was only when she returned with two steaming mugs that she realised this would probably be the last time they had coffee together. Somehow the thought was not appealing. She should be pleased to get back to normal, she thought; pleased and happy to say goodbye to all this cycling nonsense.

But how about saying goodbye to Tom — how happy would she be about that?

Well, he was bossy, irritating, and had a way of looking at her which made her feel a bit, well . . . strange inside; not horrible exactly, but disturbed. No, she had to be honest with herself. She did find him disturbing. Disturbingly attractive. More than attractive, actually. More exciting or compelling, perhaps, than attractive. In fact, if he had made a move, she had to admit to herself, she would have found it nigh on impossible to resist him.

Just as well he hadn't, really. Things were quite complicated enough as they were.

'What?' said Tom.

'I didn't say anything.'

'I know, but you were staring at me as though I'd just escaped from a zoo.'

'Well, you said it. Actually, I was just thinking that really it's been quite fun, in a strange way. I'm going to miss you.' Now why had she said that?

He gave her a crooked grin. 'Not going soft on me, are you?'

'Of course not!' said Laurie, bristling immediately. 'Don't worry, DI Jessop. You're so not my type. Too policeman-like.'

'You're not mine either. Too rebellious. But yes, it has had its moments, and I suppose I'll miss you too — in a weird way.'

The stinging retort she was searching for died on her lips because somehow she found herself looking deeply and drowningly into eyes which although were as intensely blue as ever, carried an expression she couldn't put a name to but made her feel quivery all over.

The small tin table that was between them seemed to shrink as Tom's arm stretched out and his hand took a firm hold on the back of her neck.

He stood up. 'Come here.'

Laurie got to her feet. 'What for?'

The table was no longer between them. 'So I can do this,' he said, wrapping his arms around her. With a small sigh she allowed her body to rest next to his. The fit was perfect.

'Easy, isn't it?' He leaned his chin on the top of her hair. 'Nice, too.'

Laurie hardly dared to breathe.

'Laurie,' he said as he tilted her face closer to his.

Those eyes. A girl could drown in

those eyes. Slowly, almost as though she had no will of her own, Laurie's lips parted and her lids half-closed.

'Laurie?' said Tom again just before his mouth came down on hers and Laurie went deaf, blind and became altogether lacking in any faculties of a functioning kind. A moment later she found herself succumbing to a kiss to end all kisses. It was soft and warm and tender. Just about everything a kiss should be.

But of course it did end. As abruptly as it had begun, the sweetness and the suddenness, the rapture and sheer deliciousness ended.

In stunned silence, their faces only inches apart, they stared at each other.

Eventually it was Laurie who recovered first. 'That wasn't meant to happen,' she said with a shaky laugh.

'Oh, I think it was,' answered Tom. 'I've been thinking about it for ages.'

'Have you really?'

'Of course I have. I'm a bloke.'

OK, so he was playing it cool. She

could do that. 'So, you think about kissing all the girls you meet?'

'No.' He grinned. 'Well, not like that, anyway.'

'Like that?'

Tom glanced away then back with a shrug. 'Well, you have to admit, it was a bit special.'

It was at this point Laurie realised that Tom's hand hadn't moved from its position at the back of her neck and it would only take the smallest pressure from him for an action replay of the kissing moment. The thought of it made her dizzy but she should pull away, she really should.

She tore her eyes from his, moved her head fractionally in an attempt to squint at her watch, then glanced up as another couple of cyclists hove into view and made to stop at the tea shop.

'Morning,' one of them said.

'Lovely day, isn't it?' answered Tom, relaxing his hand from Laurie's neck. Feeling suddenly weak, Laurie sat down.

A car was approaching. Still reeling from the effect of Tom's kiss, Laurie focused hazily on the driver, who appeared to be slowing down.

Despite the dark glasses, something about him looked familiar.

Oh no!

Thank goodness she was sitting down, because she'd stopped breathing and felt as though she would faint at any moment. The driver was a thick-set individual with a shaved head, and huge triceps bulging out of a tight T-shirt, and his dark glasses were directed straight towards her. Quickly, she turned her face so only her profile was visible.

From the corner of her eye she watched as the guy stared at Tom's back and the two new cyclists who were chatting companionably about the weather, the rotten rain yesterday, and how thank goodness it was so much more promising today. None of them spared the car or its driver a glance. Even so, for a terrible moment Laurie thought he was going to stop. Feeling the colour drain from her face, she sat not daring to move, even for her sunglasses, until the car had disappeared in the direction from which she and Tom had travelled.

Struggling for calm, she continued to sit as though made out of stone.

'You OK?'

The cyclists had gone into the shop to buy cold drinks, and Tom was looking at her as though she'd grown two heads or something.

'I can't believe you didn't notice . . . '

'What?'

'The car that slowed down . . . It was him.'

'Who?'

'Mickey Mouse. Who d'you think?'

A sudden light of comprehension dawned in Tom's eyes. 'Not Snake-tattoo?'

'Yes, Snake-tattoo. Same car, same T-shirt, shaved head — it's him.'

'Which way did he go?'

Laurie pointed in the direction they'd come from.

'Thank goodness for that. He's just

looking, then. Making a sweep of the area. He's not on to us yet. Hasn't even thought we might be making for the station . . . But why is he still looking? I don't understand it. He had us at the pub; he could have waited for us to show up and made his move then. What's he playing at?'

But Laurie was already explaining it to herself. 'He must have thought we were a group. The fact we were cyclists made him notice us but, although he slowed down and had a good look, he assumed it was four cyclists together, so it couldn't be us . . . Of course, he doesn't know what you look like anyway, and he probably only caught the side of my face. My hair's different and I was sitting down . . . ' Laurie got shakily to her feet. 'Oh Tom, I thought we'd got rid of him.'

Tom pulled her closer to him until their sides were touching. He hadn't worn aftershave today, but he still smelled good, thought Laurie inconsequentially. Sort of familiar and Tom-like. He put an arm round her shoulders and gave her a comforting squeeze.

'It's less than a mile to the station now, and there's a train to Chelmsford due not long after we get there. We'll be fine. Don't worry, I'm with you. What's going to happen while I'm with you, eh?'

'D'you think he'll come back?' asked Laurie through teeth that badly wanted to chatter.

'What, this way? Why should he? He thinks he's covered it already. No, we'll be fine. Now, on your bike for the final leg.'

For a moment Laurie contemplated throwing a wobbly involving heel-drumming, cycle helmet-throwing, and possibly even tears, but Tom seemed calm. He *was* calm, she thought, stealing a sideways look. Did nothing get him down? Wishing *she* felt more confident, Laurie reached for her cycle helmet and the rucksack she had thought was hers but, now it seemed, wasn't, and walked unsteadily towards her bike.

Before leaving the pub Tom had checked his phone for the time of their train. He knew that once they reached the station they'd be safe. Then it was just a question of getting Laurie and the bikes back home. In due course, the law would find Gemma's killer and justice would be done.

He should ring the station, he knew that. But what was he going to say? By sheer coincidence, he'd just bumped into Laurie in the coffee shop across the road to her flat; they were both going in the same direction, so decided to join forces? That part at least was true; but in conjunction with all the other unlikely events that had happened since, he knew a certain amount of scepticism on the part of his colleagues would surface. But what else could he have done? he asked himself. Laurie was a damsel in distress. What other recourse did he have other than to try to help her?

And the fact that she's one hell of a looker, and you really, really were attracted to her from the off, had nothing whatsoever to do with it, said the cynical part of his brain.

And that was another thing to beat himself up about. Although the tantalising sight of her in her stretchy leggings and well-fitting T-shirts had been driving him nuts, and the sheer proximity of sharing a room with her had pushed his every primitive male urge to breaking point, he'd managed to resist and be professional enough to keep things business-like and his behaviour above reproach. So whyever, when they were on the last leg of the journey, did he permit himself that off-guard moment and give into the romantic instinct to kiss her?

You idiot, Tom. You were nearly home and dry. He gave an ironic grin. It was worth it though, and it hadn't complicated matters as much as he'd thought it might. He owed that to the fact of the other two cyclists turning up.

That made it two reasons for being thankful to them.

The station was in sight now. 'How're you doing?' he called back over his shoulder to Laurie.

There was no answer. He knew there was no traffic behind him so he pulled over and waited.

A couple of moments went by and there was still no sign of her. Where was she? There was a bend in the road behind him. Perhaps with everything that was going on in his head, he'd gone faster than he'd intended. He carried on waiting.

But what if . . . ?

What if Snake-tattoo had got her? Sweating slightly and suddenly very scared, Tom turned his bike and started swiftly cycling back the way he had come. It could have happened, of course it could. It wouldn't take a minute to pull up in front of her, force her to dismount, bundle her into the car, then take off again, leaving the bike on the grass verge.

And what had he been doing? Just cycling away, thinking idle thoughts about kissing a girl who was well out of his league, while all the time said girl could be in real danger. Tom started to sweat some more and his heart rate increased to a pace that had nothing to do with the speed of his cycling.

He turned the bend and there it was as though preordained — her bike abandoned on the grass verge, its back wheel still spinning.

There was nothing in sight. Just a fence and a few scrubby bushes, then a farmer's field with nothing going on in it as far as Tom could see. Panic overtook him.

'Oh God,' said Tom, feeling the ghastly shiver of fear travel down his spine. He stared at the empty road. He was a fast cyclist but even he knew he had no hope of catching a car. He didn't know its number or even the make or colour. Whatever had happened to his policing abilities? Well that settled it; he'd have to phone for assistance, admit he'd made a botch of the whole thing and get the search for Laurie underway.

'Hello there.' Laurie's head popped out from behind a bush. 'Sorry, did you wonder where I was? Had to spend a penny, I'm afraid. Just couldn't wait a moment longer.' She broke off. 'You look a bit pale. You all right?'

'What the . . . ?' shouted Tom, who had seldom felt so furious.

'What's the matter? I tried to call after you, but you'd gone so far so quickly, you didn't hear me.'

'It didn't occur to you I might be worried?'

'No,' said Laurie. 'Why should you be?'

'Snake-tattoo?' He leaned over and pulled her bike upright. 'Never mind. Just come on, let's get to the station.'

With tight lips Laurie got on her bike. He thought he heard her say something derogatory about the male sex in general and Tom in particular. And then go on about how typical it was for a man to make such a ridiculous fuss over nothing, and anyway, what else did he expect her to do in the circumstances?

Secretly and absurdly grateful that his fears had been unfounded and she was unharmed, he made no sign of having heard her enraged rant.

Get to the station, catch the train, phone the station and take her straight in for questioning and formal body identification. Yes, that was the way to play it.

By the book.

Wishing he was feeling happier about it, Tom pedalled on.

* * *

What a fuss, thought Laurie. If it had been him who'd had to disappear behind a hedge for a moment of privacy, would she have carried on as though the world was at an end? Of course not. She blinked hard and gritted her teeth. The truth was that Tom suddenly shouting at her had nearly been her undoing. She had so nearly burst into tears. And why not? The last few days had been exhausting, not only physically but mentally too. A girl deserved a little bit of peace and quiet, a little bit of consideration and tact, a little bit of TLC, surely?

Well, she wasn't going to get it from DI Jessop, that was for sure. Just because he'd kissed her, and told her it had been special, that meant nothing in his police notebook. Stupid as she was, she'd allowed herself to think just for a moment that maybe he did have some feelings for her. *Well, wrong again Laurie.* Clearly!

They had reached the station now. Laurie dismounted and took off her cycle helmet. Briefly she wondered about its last owner. Had Tom shouted at her for no reason too?

Apologising to the station officials for not checking earlier that there was room, Tom arranged for the bikes to go on the train. Luckily there was space, and when the train came in, Tom together with a train person or whatever they were called these days stowed them on board. At this time of day the train was pretty empty, and they found seats opposite one another in an almost empty compartment.

'Great,' said Tom, removing his helmet and running a hand over his dark hair. 'Now we need to get your story straight.'

Briefly, Laurie closed her eyes. She really didn't want to do this anymore. 'What d'you mean, 'straight'? You make it sound as though I'm lying.'

'No, it's just that people get confused, especially after a time lapse and when a lot of other things have gone on. Look, Laurie, I've told you — it won't be me interviewing you, and you need to get certain facts, certain times straight in your mind.'

'Why? Why won't it be you interviewing me?'

'Because the body's been found. There'll be a new investigating officer. They won't wait for me. It is, after all, a murder investigation.'

Murder investigation. The words echoed round in Laurie's brain. She licked lips that were suddenly dry. 'Sorry,' she said. Then her fighting spirit came back with a force that surprised her. 'But right now I'm so tired I don't even know what day it is. I can't, I just *can't* go over all this stuff yet again — and how many times do I have to tell you *I don't know anything anyway!*'

'OK, OK,' said Tom, glancing round nervously. 'It's only day one you've got to think about anyway, and the morning of day two I suppose. I've been with you since then.'

Laurie sighed. 'OK.' She screwed up her eyes in thought. 'I'd arranged to have a half-day and the rest of the week off, because the day previously I'd had a call from my friend Gemma that she was now in the UK and would like to stay for a few days until she went to visit relatives up north. Don't know where or what relatives; she didn't say. Don't know when she arrived; she didn't say. I'd told her where I lived and that there was a spare key under the mat. When I reached home, early afternoon, my door was open and I could hear Snake-tattoo talking on the phone — something about how he'd been disturbed but was still looking. I was uneasy, thought he was a burglar or something, and as quietly as possible went back to the lobby in order to phone the police. Before I could do so, Snake-tattoo started down the stairs. I hid in a cupboard.' Goodness, she was starting to get the hang of this policeman-speak now.

'OK, I know the next bit,' said Tom. 'Run through what you did after Morgan and I left.'

'I spotted Gemma's hold-all. In all the fuss I hadn't noticed it stuck beside my sofa. Somehow a dead body appearing and disappearing in the space of half an hour or so had put it clear out of my mind.'

'Just the facts, Laurie, please.'

'Right, so I went through it. Just dirty

washing and a couple of books, I think. Anyway, the bag's probably still there — you can see for yourself.' She frowned rather suddenly. 'D'you think he might have gone through it? Hey,' she said, her face brightening, 'there might have been drugs in the spine of a book. How about that?'

'I think we've established that it was the rucksack he was after all the time, so it seems doubtful.'

'Hmm,' said a disappointed Laurie. 'Well, I was still very frightened about staying there for the night. After all, I knew there'd been a dead body, even though the police didn't believe me; I knew I was of perfectly sound mind and not given to imagining things of that nature. Kathy, my neighbour, is away this week, so I had her key in order to feed Sonny and Cher, her goldfish. So I packed a bag, took my rucksack and slept at hers for the night. Brilliant, hey? Good job I did, too, because next morning I was having breakfast in the café across the road from the flats when who should turn up? Snake-tattoo, that's who. He stood outside the café, obviously watching my flat for any signs of life before going over there — for another search, I suppose — and that's probably when he took my camera. You know the rest. What d'you say, me lord? Guilty or not guilty?'

'It's the truth, isn't it? So just stick to it. Don't deviate. They'll ask you to be more specific. Be as clear-minded as you can be. They'll probably ask a lot more about Gemma, but don't tell me now; I want you to answer as naturally as you possibly can when the time comes. I don't want you to sound as though you've rehearsed it.'

'So why make me go through the other bit again?'

Tom sighed and rubbed his eyes which, she suddenly noticed, had dark shadows beneath them. 'I don't know. Thought it might help, I suppose.'

'D'you think, bearing in mind he took my camera, that he's after some kind of SD card, some sort of photographic evidence of something? Perhaps there was a teeny, tiny one in that seam I unpicked and I missed it?'

Tom stared at her long and hard. 'Grit,' he said suddenly. 'Grit. South Africa! I'm an idiot.'

'What?' said Laurie. 'What are you on about?'

'The grit that you thought was silicon — it was knobbly and uncomfortable, you said. Must have been more like gravel than silicon to be that uncomfortable. Where did you put it?'

'What?'

'The grit.'

Laurie shrugged. 'Threw it away, I suppose.'

Tom gave a groan and covered his face with his hands.

10

'You've got your axe murderer's face on again.'

'Where? Where did you throw it away?'

Laurie shrugged. 'In the bin, I expect. Where else?'

'How long ago?'

'I dunno . . . Oh, ages. When I first came back from Jo'berg, probably.'

Tom put his head back in his hands. 'Marvellous,' he said. 'So it's gone out with the rubbish then. So we're floored, stymied.'

'Don't see why it's so important,' said Laurie sulkily, 'but actually, no . . . In thinking about it, I believe I might have put it in the plant pot.' She frowned as if re-visualising the scene. 'I was sitting on the sofa at the time. I'd just unpicked the seam and taken the silica grit out. I started sewing the seam up again so I just put the grit on top of the cabinet and forgot about it. Then later on I was doing a bit of dusting, and the grit was just sitting there — so I picked it up and stuck it with the other grit on the aloe vera.'

Tom did a quick recall of Laurie's sitting room. 'The plant pot on the cabinet, the cactus with the half-dead leaves? Please tell me it wasn't one you've since thrown out.'

'Well, I must admit I was thinking about it, but that's the trouble with living in a flat — nowhere to throw things like that out. I really feel it should be recycled somehow, but of course, I don't have a compost heap. Impossible in a flat . . . ' She broke off. 'What are you looking at me like that for?'

Tom could hardly contain his impatience. 'You're telling me it's still there then?'

'Yes, it must be. Actually it's perked up a bit lately; perhaps the dried silica did it good. I suppose it could contain some kind of mineral — good for the soil. Although with aloe vera, you tear a bit off and use the sap to soothe a burn. That's why I got it, really, as I'm always burning myself on the grill shelf because I haven't got a toaster.'

'Stop giving me a lecture on gardening and cooking and listen for once.'

'That's unfair. I always listen,' said Laurie hotly.

'OK, you're not feeling very bright today. I'll spell it out for you. *South Africa, grit, smuggling*. What does that equal?'

Her eyes widening in sudden comprehension, Laurie stared back at him. 'Not . . . not *diamonds*, as in sparkly?'

'Yes, got to be. Can't be anything else. A few little bits of grit, aka *diamonds*, could be worth a fortune. It explains everything, doesn't it? Why Snake-tattoo went to your flat in the first place. Why he took the rucksack. Why, when he realised his mistake, he came back next morning looking for the other one. And why he's been looking for you and it ever since. Why he switched them again and why he's still looking for you even as we speak. Well, doesn't it?'

'Crikey,' said Laurie. 'Hold on. So how did that work, then? What about Gemma?'

'Suppose Gemma was a small part of a smuggling ring and was used to transport them from A to B, but somehow your rucksack and hers got switched or confused.'

'Switched?'

'Maybe not deliberately, even. Maybe when she realised what had happened, she panicked and ran. Perhaps it took a long time for them to catch up with her, or perhaps she went into hiding waiting for the fuss to die down before coming after you to retrieve them. She probably figured they'd be safe where they were, with you not even realising the rucksack was different.'

Laurie was frowning. 'Or more likely she switched them deliberately . . . Perhaps that was why she insisted on buying the same rucksack as me in the first place. It was probably why she insisted on seeing me off at the airport — to make sure I got out safely — and then it was obviously why she kept in contact with me.' She paused. 'I thought that was strange. OK, so I stayed with her for a bit and it was good of her to take me in, but I paid my way and we never were what you might call buddies.'

'Never mind all that,' said Tom impatiently. 'Suppose the other members of the gang caught up with her and she told them what had happened. That must be it! She used you as her get-out clause, pretending it was all a terrible mistake; but hey, she could get your English address! As a delaying tactic she might have said she'd have to contact one of your friends in Jo'berg in order to get it, or possibly even gave them a contact so they could find it themselves. After all, she could claim to have hardly known you, so why would she have kept in touch? She'd point out that it would be simple for their contacts in London to stage a burglary this end. And, oh look, Laurie had done her smuggling for her — albeit innocently! Brilliant!'

'Or it was, until she tried to beat them to it!'

'She must have already planned to come here and, in an effort to beat the contacts this end, she skipped as soon as she'd spun her story. If by chance she didn't beat them, oh well, some you win, some you lose. You have to hand it to her, she was one smart cookie.'

'Of all the nerve,' said Laurie. 'I can't believe she'd do that to me. If I'd got caught at customs, she'd be in the clear and I'd be banged up!'

Ignoring the swaying of the train, which had picked up speed, Tom leaned towards her. 'But why would you be caught? You'd never be suspected or searched. Your first trip to South Africa, with a boyfriend, on a fashion shoot? I don't think so. You'd have no contacts, nothing. If she planned it — and I think you're right about that — the whole thing's brilliant! She waved you off to England and kept in contact, but only loosely. Then she turns up out of the blue, with her rucksack, intending to either switch them back again immediately or just remove the stones from yours. If Snake-tattoo has beaten her to it, she's still free to disappear again to see her 'relatives' in the north of England.'

'I'll bet she doesn't even have any relatives in England. I never heard her mention them before.'

'Probably not. Her whole plan from the outset was to double-cross her gang. More than likely she was going to hop over to Amsterdam, do a deal, pocket the money and vanish, never to be seen again. You've got to hand it to her, she was pretty clever.'

'Yes, in a sneaky, unprincipled way,' said Laurie, smarting slightly at the note of admiration in Tom's voice.

But before he could ponder for too long on the faint possibility that she was experiencing something akin to jealousy, the train juddered and slowed, causing his knee to jolt forward onto hers. Avoiding his gaze, she moved her leg away and continued. 'But her timing was out. One of the gang's contacts got to me first. Or actually, a bit of rough justice here — he got to *her* first. Snake-tattoo came whilst I was out, rucksack and all; but Gemma had arrived with hers, so it seems like he killed the wrong girl and took the wrong rucksack! Poor Gemma!'

'It was probably accidental,' said Tom. 'His only intention was to pinch the rucksack. Maybe she fought him a bit too hard. She fell awkwardly, broke her neck, and he had a body on his hands.'

Laurie's eyes were opening wider and wider. 'So he wasn't looking for me *personally* after all — just the rucksack. He knew he had to get out of there fast, so off he went, thinking he'd got the right rucksack and the diamonds but *the flat owner*, one Laurie Kendal, was now dead. There was nothing to tell him Gemma wasn't still in Jo'berg. That was what he meant by 'got it'; that was what he meant by 'clear-up job'.'

'Yes, of course. It wouldn't have been until later when he realised that Gemma was up to some tricky business, but the best thing all round then would be to hot-foot it out of there and arrange for the body to be moved. Two-man job: wrap her in your rug and out through the fire escape at the back of the building. You said yourself that there's no one around at that time of day. We must have just missed them.'

'How awful. Poor Gemma!' said Laurie again. 'Wait a minute. Why, when he came back next day . . . Why did he take my camera?'

Tom shrugged. 'Because the man's a tea leaf. Greedy, like all thieves. Couldn't resist it. There was nothing else worth taking, and who would know?'

'Bloomin' nerve,' said Laurie. 'I loved that camera.'

Grinning widely, Tom stretched back in his seat.

'What do we do now?' asked Laurie.

'I've got some serious phoning to do. I'll have to do some explaining at the station. I think the best bet is to arrange to have a police presence outside your flat from now on. We'll take the bikes straight to your flat; they'll be safe there. Hopefully we'll retrieve the diamonds, you can go through your story again, and I'll be there to back you up.'

'What about Snake-tattoo?' asked Laurie in a subdued tone. 'It's all very well, but he knows my name and what I look like now; he knows where I live and in his book, I've still got the diamonds. Not very nice from where I'm sitting!'

'The police presence will be low-key. We'll be watching for him. If he shows up there he'll be apprehended, I promise you.'

Laurie giggled.

'What's funny?'

'You. You're doing it again. 'Police presence', 'apprehended' . . . It's so *The Bill*.'

285

Tom consulted his mobile. 'OK, you've had your laugh. Now it's serious. I've got to report. Please just try and keep quiet while I do my job.'

★ ★ ★

OK, she could take a hint. Laurie sat quietly, trying not to feel too impressed as she listened and watched Tom, with his serious Mr Plod face on, speak quietly and succinctly into the phone, giving a precise and somewhat doctored account of the last few days to his superior and then, in a tone that was slightly more authoritative, to his colleagues.

As he spoke, Laurie found herself remembering with perfect clarity how much she'd enjoyed teasing him, laughing with him, and how much she'd come to rely on him to just be there with a smile or dry comment every time she felt low or unsure of how this was all going to end. Then she allowed herself to realise that, when this was all over, she would miss him.

She would miss him a lot.

She sighed, squared her shoulders and, as Tom had suggested, concentrated on visualising Snake-tattoo's description ready for her interview with the police artist. Then she whiled away some time checking her messages and found a few from friends wondering where she was, what she was doing and when they'd see her back down the pub. 'Doing OK C U soon,' she texted everyone. There was one message from her dad on voice mail. 'Catch up with you soon, Laurie. Mum said you'd called. I'll be home Saturday so Sunday would be good.'

In the unlikely event of them meeting, what would Dad think of Tom? she wondered.

What would Tom think of her dad? They might get on OK. They could probably manage a decent sporting conversation. She didn't think Tom would score so well on the big business talk, though. Her breath caught in her throat as she reminded herself that once this was over she'd never set eyes on DI Tom Jessop again, so she had just better accept it.

Anyway, she should be feeling scared about the here and now; terrified that Snake-tattoo would still catch up with them — not obsessing about never seeing Tom again. She was tough, wasn't she? She'd handled breaking up with guys who'd been real romantic contenders and whom she'd known far longer than Tom. Oh yes, she could handle saying goodbye to DI Jessop perfectly well.

Tom had put his mobile away now and, with barely a glance at her, leaned across to peer out of the window. 'Nearly there,' he said with a lift to his voice just as though he couldn't wait to get this all done and dusted, so he never had to see her again as long as he lived. 'Only the Underground now. It was suggested we leave our bikes at one of the stations, but my bike? No way! We'll take them with us. Tube won't be too full at this time of day.'

His bike was of far more importance to him than she was. Clearly!

A fat tear slid down Laurie's cheek.

'What's up?' Tom was staring as her with concern in his intense blue eyes. 'Look, you don't have to worry. The team are on to it. They'll find Snake-tattoo. He's undoubtedly got form. You'll recognise him from an identikit portrait, and they're probably running through the records right now for diamond smugglers and the like.' He gave a crooked smile. 'We've got all the modern technology. He won't get far. He certainly won't get you, so don't be scared.' He put his hand on her arm and gave it a squeeze that was disappointingly brotherly.

'I'm not scared,' said Laurie with indignation befitting a sister, if that was how he wanted to play it. 'I think I'm allowed a little wobble after the last few days.'

'Oh undoubtedly,' said Tom. 'Undoubtedly . . . You've been good as gold really, under the circumstances.'

And that, thought Laurie, was as near to a compliment as she was ever likely to get.

* * *

The Underground was easy. Tom sat back against the back of the train seat. It hadn't been as bad as he'd feared. And his fears had been pretty realistic. For once Snake-tattoo had found the diamonds weren't in either rucksack, it couldn't have taken him too long to figure out the likelihood that Laurie had discovered and removed them. That made her a target on three counts. She'd crossed the gang, stolen the diamonds and, above all, although they didn't know exactly how much she knew, it was obvious she knew way too much. It wouldn't occur to him that she might mistake uncut diamonds for bits of silica and thrown them away.

He smiled at the thought. What an innocent she was, and what a Dumbo he'd been. Why hadn't he thought of diamonds straight away? It seemed so obvious now. He'd said as much to the super, who'd been far more understanding than he'd expected — even mentioned the word 'initiative', which was rare, *and* in connection to *Tom's* part in all this, which was even rarer.

'Are you requesting back-up when you arrive?' he'd asked.

'Don't see the point in drawing attention to ourselves,' Tom said. 'Even if they've sussed we're making our way back to Laurie's flat, they wouldn't attempt anything on the Underground.'

'She's an important witness.'

'I realise that, sir.'

'Take care of her.'

'Oh, I will do, sir.' Perhaps he'd been overly emphatic on that.

'What's going on, exactly?' asked Laurie, bringing him back to the present and the realisation that they weren't quite home and dry yet. She seemed to have perked up a bit now. Earlier on he'd thought she might lose it and start with the waterworks, which he wouldn't have blamed her for really. But he was glad all the same that she hadn't.

'Two plainclothes constables will check and watch your flat until we arrive. Any sign of other interest will be noted. Once we're in there we'll examine the plant pot, put the whole thing in an evidence bag, and a car will take us to the station leaving the plainclothes officers at the site.'

'What about the bikes?'

Tom laughed; she never ceased to surprise him. 'We'll leave them in your hall. They'll be fine. They'd better be. Mine's worth a fortune!'

'More than the diamonds? I don't think so!'

'It's going to be a long haul,' went on Tom. 'Interviews, paperwork, etcetera. I wish I could spare you.' He half-expected her to say something about if he'd believed her in the first place, he wouldn't have to spare her from anything. But she didn't; she just turned her head to the window so that he could only see her profile against the dark of the tunnel.

It was a good profile: a sweep of hair

exposing a high forehead and one strong eyebrow, an eye with a fringe of dark lashes tipped with gold, a nose that was ordinary, not too big or small, nostrils clearly defined but hardly chiselled. Then came her upper lip, which curled slightly, but her mouth with its full lower lip was nothing short of perfection. Tom knew that mouth; could remember the blissful feel of it beneath his own. Recalling the sensation, he swallowed and wondered how on earth, when this was all over, he would ever manage without her.

★　★　★

'Can you pick out the bits you found in the rucksack, Laurie?'

Laurie looked helplessly at the plant pot in front of her. 'Hang on a minute. I told you it just looked like grit. Perhaps it was just grit. Perhaps we're wrong.'

'We're not wrong,' said Tom. 'We can't be wrong.'

Judith Morgan peered over her shoulder. 'Those bits there,' she said, poking her finger at some pieces of what looked like gravel towards the back of the plant. 'They look bigger and slightly less pink. I think it might be those.'

'Really?' said Laurie. 'Well, yes, I suppose they might be, but I've only ever seen shiny diamonds, and not too many of those I'm afraid.'

'Well . . . ' Tom carefully put the pot containing the half-dead aloe vera plus soil and grit into an incident bag. 'We'll let the experts have a look when we get to the station.'

'Right.' Laurie was feeling slightly more confident now. Judith Morgan had been quite nice to her, in a professional way; she'd understood, too, when Laurie had insisted she go next door and feed Sonny and Cher, who were still swimming around in their tank looking no thinner than before. The other plainclothes constable was big and beefy, and his presence added to Tom's made Laurie feel safe and even rather special. A nice change, she thought, from feeling like a nuisance on a par with an annoying mosquito.

When they arrived at the station she was immediately swept up in police procedure, which she found baffling yet reassuring at the same time. She told her story several times, then signed a statement. The bag containing the plant and hopefully the diamonds had been whisked away. Laurie didn't care; she didn't particularly ever want to see it again. Then she was taken on another car journey, this time to a different police station, in order to identify Gemma's body.

'Don't be scared,' said Tom, who wasn't coming with her. 'It's quite simple. You just have to say whether it's Gemma or not. Oh, and also identify the rug.'

'Actually, I don't really want the rug back.'

Tom gave her a half-smile — the one she liked so much. 'Understandable. But identify it all the same — if it's yours, that is.'

Unable to believe that this was really happening, Laurie allowed herself to be taken into a small room where the body was lying covered with a sheet. She took a deep breath, then nodded that she was ready for the cover to be lifted.

It was Gemma. She looked exactly as dead bodies appeared on television programmes. Her hair was in a mass around her face, which looked pale and peaceful. Once she'd been so full of life; annoying, but full of life. And now . . . nothing. There was no one there. Just an empty casing.

The reality of it sinking in, Laurie blinked. It could so easily be her lying there on a cold slab. She took a long last look and nodded.

After signing another form and on a promise of a cup of tea when she arrived back at the station to go through another identification procedure, she climbed on wobbly legs back into the police car for the return journey.

The cup of tea made her feel a little better.

'I suppose you must get used to it,' she said to Tom.

'Well, not exactly used to it, but it gets easier, yes.'

Laurie shuddered. 'I just want to get this over with,' she said. 'And I then I want to go home.'

'Sorry, not just yet. We want you to look at some photos.'

She sighed. 'OK.'

★   ★   ★

'That's him!'

Laurie could hardly believe it. After what seemed like hours of answering questions and examining photos flashed up on computer, she was staring at the face of Snake-tattoo. Although she'd only snatched a brief glance from within a dark cupboard, she was certain it was him. 'That's the man I saw at my flat,' she said again, so there could be no mistake.

'It fits,' said Tom, who was there even though he'd thought it wouldn't be allowed. 'Fits his profile to a T. All we've got to do now is track him down.'

'Oh, that's all!'

'Oh, ye of little faith. You'd be surprised. We'll get him, and soon.'

'Meanwhile, what do I do? Sit in my flat as bait?' She'd said it as a joke because that was the one thing she was not going to do, but she saw Tom's eyes widen as the possibility of the idea overtook him.

'No, Morgan's doing that — along with back-up,' said another detective who looked as though he lived on burgers and cigarettes. Laurie hadn't worked out what rank he held yet, but hoped it wasn't anything which required him to run fast.

'Right, we'd best put her in a safe house,' said the officer whom Tom referred to as the 'super'.

Tom looked up. 'She's staying with a friend. She'll be safe there.' Laurie opened her mouth to protest. 'I'll take her myself,' went on Tom after a warning look in her direction.

Laurie closed her mouth again. So he wasn't giving up on her quite yet. It wasn't finished. It wasn't over. A warm feeling started in the pit of her stomach and her heart beat a little faster.

He used a police car — or 'vehicle' as, back in full police-speak mode, he called it. By this time Laurie was so tired she could barely think, let alone speak. She knew they were going to Tom's place; knew that somehow their bike panniers and her rucksack were in the back, so at least she'd have a toothbrush. She sat in the passenger seat and rested her head against the window. Not a comfortable position for sleep, but she must have dozed off because the next thing she knew Tom was helping her out of the car and up the stairs to his flat.

'I hope you've brought me up here in order to have your evil way with me,' she mumbled, only half-awake. 'Oh no, that's not what I meant. I meant I hope you *didn't . . . Didn't* want to have your evil way with me.'

Tom chuckled. 'No question about that. Of course I *want* to. But not on duty. I'm surprised you could even think of such a thing!'

'I wasn't,' said Laurie, as befuddled as

ever. 'I was joking, but it came out wrong.'

Tom grinned. 'Good. So was I. Joking, I mean.'

She punched his arm. He winced as he put his key in the lock and the door swung open. 'I wish you'd stop doing that. My arm's got bruises from shoulder to elbow.'

'Well, I never know when you're serious. You're the most annoying person I've ever known.'

'Oh, I can be more annoying than that, I promise you.' He pushed her into the sitting room and dumped her panniers in the bedroom. 'I'll take the sofa, you can have the bed.'

'That's kind. Thanks.' Fully awake now, she rubbed at her arm, which had gone to sleep in the car.

'I've got bacon and eggs in the fridge, baked beans in the cupboard, and I can do black coffee. That's it, I'm afraid.'

Laurie was struggling to push her arms into a sweater she'd had round her shoulders. 'Sounds fine. Lovely! D'you want some help?'

'You can watch and encourage if you like.'

Another surprise for Laurie: Tom was quite at home in the kitchen. That was due to his mother, he explained; coming from a large family they all had to learn the basics. 'Mum always worked, even if not full time, so we all had to muck in — put our dirty clothes in the bin, hang up the towels, know how to make a quick meal out of nothing. I'm very good at ironing shirts too.'

Knowing the limitations of her own domestic abilities, Laurie said nothing; just watched as Tom scrambled eggs, fried bacon, defrosted two crusty rolls and made black coffee in next to no time. She found some cutlery and a couple of plates, and soon they were sitting opposite the TV balancing their makeshift meal on their laps, with two mugs of steaming coffee on the low table in front of them.

'That was good,' she said when they'd finally finished. 'I didn't realise I was so hungry.'

'It's been a long day,' said Tom.

'D'you mind if I watch the news?'

The sofa, despite being leather — which Laurie usually associated with being too hot in summer and too cold in winter — turned out to be quite comfortable. Yawning, she curled up in one corner with her legs tucked under her. 'I hope I don't drop off,' was the last thing she remembered saying before being aware of the ring of a phone.

She struggled awake. Her head was on a pillow Tom must have fetched from the bedroom; there'd been no sign of a cushion in Tom's masculine sitting room. Her legs were out flat, resting on a pair of knees. The owner of the knees was talking excitedly into his mobile. 'Good,' he was saying. 'Excellent . . . Great work . . . Wish I'd been there . . . Evidence, yes. Really? Didn't expect that . . . So, they'll be looking for links in Jo'berg? Did he? That figures.' He turned his head and registered that Laurie was awake now. 'Right, great. Yep, talk to you later.' He clicked off.

'What?' Excitedly, Laurie swung her

legs to the floor and sat up.

'They've got him.'

'Snake-tattoo?'

'Yep, and his mates. The grit *is* diamonds, by the way. It was a small operation in the end, but Snake-tattoo sang like a canary.' He grinned. 'Never guess what — got your camera too! That's evidence that he was in your flat. Evidence apart from yours, that is.'

Half-crying from relief, Laurie hugged herself. 'I never thought it would be so quick.'

'Neither did I, to be truthful.'

'I can go home then?'

'Well, in theory, or . . . '

'Or what?'

He grinned. 'Or, we could stay here and party.'

Laurie let that one sink in. Why did she suddenly feel shaky, as though she couldn't quite meet Tom's eyes? 'I'm not sure I like parties.'

Tom waited until she ventured a brief glance from under her lids. His eyes were very blue, very steady. 'Neither am

I usually, but I'm pretty sure we'll like this one.'

Laurie's heart was thudding so loudly she was sure he must be able to hear it. 'Do you mean what I think you mean?'

'Depends what you think I mean, but yes, I think I do.'

'But we argue all the time — don't we?'

Tom drew back with a look of fury on his face. 'How dare you say that?' he thundered. Then grinned again. 'Only joking.'

'So you do quite like me, then?'

'Oh yes, I like you. I like the way you make a fuss about tiny things but take on great big ones as though they're nothing at all. I like your gutsiness. You never murmured about having your hair cut, or getting knocked off your bike, or getting freezing cold and soaking wet, besides being half-scared out of your wits. I like that you get my jokes, and the way you talk utter nonsense one moment and the next you're laughing like a drain.' He traced her lips with his finger. 'I like your smile; I like your fierce eyebrows. In fact, I think what I'm trying to say is . . . that I've fallen very seriously in like with you. The question is, do you like me too?'

Laurie smiled because suddenly everything seemed right. 'Oh yes, Mr Plod. You have no idea . . . I've definitely fallen in like with you too!'

'Laurie, strictly speaking, I'm not on this case anymore.' He put an arm round her shoulders and pulled her close to him. 'But strictly speaking, I shouldn't be doing this either, although I'm going to anyway . . . unless you have some violent objection. Do you?'

His lips came closer. 'No,' said Laurie, leaning in for his kiss. 'I don't have any objections at all. Absolutely none.'

THE END